# BOUND to DARKNESS

USA TODAY BESTSELLING AUTHOR
## J.L. BECK
NEW YORK TIMES BESTSELLING AUTHOR
## MONICA CORWIN

Copyright © 2022 by Bleeding Heart Press

www.bleedingheartpress.com

Cover design by C. Hallman

Cover image taken by Wander Aguiar

Cover model: Jeff

All rights reserved.

No part of this book may be reproduced in any form or by any electronic or mechanical means, including information storage and retrieval systems, without written permission from the author, except for the use of brief quotations in a book review.

# 1

## KAI

*I*t's quiet in the dark. Fuck, I haven't had this much silence in my life for years. It almost makes my ears ring. Every heartbeat seems to pulse in that noise until I take a long deep breath and let it out slowly. This isn't the first time I've been cornered, and it won't be the last.

My cell is a solid, thick kind of concrete, so there's no getting out of it until I'm released. So I wait. Adrian and Valentina won't let me rot in here. For all the things I've done, I trust them with my life.

Dried blood crusts on my jaw, but I don't waste the little water they've given me by washing it off. My knuckles are bruised from fighting the bastards, but I couldn't do much while being held down with someone's knee in my back as they battered me black and blue for answers.

My mouth twists into a smile. There's no way in hell they'll be able to drag the answers out of me. That's something they don't understand.

I scrub at the dried blood, now itchy, with the heel of my hand. Which is pretty much the only part of my body not bruised.

When I took my friend's place on the chopping block, the council promised mercy, and I suppose not putting a bullet in my head immediately after my confession was their form of leniency. These people don't know the meaning of mercy.

And when I get out of this cell, I won't be the one to teach it to them.

It's been a week by my estimation, hazy though it is. The only time I'm actually alert is during the short window in which they drag me out of the cell, hose me down, feed me a Viagra, and strap me to the head councilwoman's bed. She's even more disgusting than I gave her credit for. Worse, she assumes everyone wants her. So even though I'm drugged and tied down, she thinks it's a seduction and not a rape.

When I get out of here, I'm going to make her pay for this and for what she orchestrated against Andrea. Her attack could only have been sanctioned by Henrietta, as she asked me to call her while she rode my dick without my fucking permission.

I close my eyes and squeeze them shut so at least I can tell myself the darkness is my choice. This is how I get through anything. Grab some part of it and make it mine. I'll get out of here and do the same.

Rose pops into my head, as she always does, and I feel myself calming and breathing deeper. It's a trick I learned when I first took her to my apartment outside the penthouse. If I stay calm, she stays calm. If she stays calm, then things don't get broken, and I don't have to cradle a crying, screaming girl for way longer than my sanity can handle.

Adrian warned me not to touch her, and I've mostly kept that promise. If I had to put my hands on her, it was for medical care or comfort and nothing more. Even if I've thought about it.

There's a sound in the hall. The problem with concrete is it echoes loudly, and I have excellent hearing. It's not the click of high heels, thank fuck, to alert me that she's asked for me again, nor is it the heavy drum bass of the guard pacing back and forth in front of my cell for the past two hours.

I think it's night. At least it feels that way by the chill in the air. I'm wearing nothing but the clean boxer briefs they gave me this morning after Henrietta was through using me. Time is harder to discern. The guards change shifts every eight hours, and there are four who regularly rotate outside my cell if their gait is anything to go by. I call one fatty with his heavy clomp clomp clomping step, and one gimpy because he has a sort of drag to his step with every turn. One is skippy since he seems to run back and forth in the hallway, moving quickly, like he is trying to get a workout in during every guard shift. The last one is the meanest, and I just call him motherfucker. His steps are normal, at least for this lot, but his fists are rougher than the others, and he's not afraid to hit me.

My guess...Henrietta had been sleeping with him before she decided to get herself an upgrade.

I focus on the steps again, but there are several now. One I'd recognize anywhere. I've been listening to them pace the halls of the penthouse for years.

I tuck my legs up to hide my nudity and brace my arms across my knees so he can't see the bruises there.

The door is thrown open, but it's not Adrian who walks in. It's Valentina. Ah. She's light, tiny, and I usually can't hear her walking around unless she's angry.

She takes a step into the cell with Adrian right on her ass. The guard closes the door behind them.

"Careful," I warn. "Now that they've got you in here, they might not let you out again."

Adrian digs his cell phone out of his pocket and flips on the flashlight so we can see each other. "This place is a shithole. Don't they know concrete isn't great for holding cells? It's too damn hard to heat."

I shiver as if proving his point, but it's more out of adrenaline from seeing them than the actual chill in the air. "What are you doing here? The live stream I did should have given you guys time to get away."

He snorts and shoves the hand not holding his phone into his pocket. "You really think I'd leave you just like that?"

I wave at his wife. "To protect Valentina and your child? Of course I do." Maybe he's fucking with me for defying his orders and coming after him even though he expressly forbade it. "And I sure as hell didn't think you'd be dumb enough to bring her back here, under any circumstance."

He meets my eyes head-on and shrugs. "It seems I can't deny her anything. Her only request every day for the past week has been to come here and get you out. Considering I also want you out of this hellhole, I was inclined to make it happen."

A bright light surges in my chest. "We're leaving?"

"Not yet," Valentina says, closing the distance between us. I stare at her, almost on equal height with me sitting on the bench and her short stature.

She strikes out, slapping me hard across the cheek. She caught a little of my ear, too, causing it to ring.

I clutch my face and glare her way. "What the hell? Haven't I been beaten enough recently?"

"Watch your tone," Adrian hisses, stepping behind her to cup her upper arms and pull her back a few steps.

"Why didn't you tell me Rose was alive?" she demands, her fists clenched at her side.

I peer over her shoulder at Adrian and answer. "Why do you think? Orders. It's the reason I do anything."

She waves around the room exaggeratedly, her arm casting shadows in Adrian's flashlight. "You seem to disobey orders just fine when it suits you, and I saved your life, or have you forgotten?"

Guilt. Another old friend threatens to choke me, but I shove it down again. "I stand by my decision to keep her existence a secret. It wasn't safe for either of you between Sal's family and your father. Besides, mentally, she still needs a lot of care. She has a hard time processing things, being touched, or even going outside. And there's one more major reason I didn't tell you."

Her hands frame her slim hips, her curls spinning around her face in her anger. "Yes?"

"She doesn't want to see you. We talked about it, and she specifically told me she doesn't want to see you."

At my admission, Valentina gasps and steps backward into Adrian's chest. He immediately folds her into his arms, the light spinning to illuminate the floor. There's only so much he can protect her from, and the truth isn't one of them.

I wait for her to get ahold of herself, praying it's sooner rather than later as I do want out of this shit box before Henrietta returns and they find out what she's been doing to me.

"Is that it?" she whispers. "Are there any other secrets I should know about? Any other lies you have hidden up your sleeve waiting to ambush me?"

I shake my head. "No. I was tasked to take her to safety and keep her safe, and that's what I've done."

She freezes, her body going rigid. "Oh, my god, she's been there all this time alone, and you haven't been able to check on her. What if she's hurt or ran out of food—?"

"I put a system in place. A cleaning lady, Parker, comes every week and delivers anything she might need in case I can't make it back to the apartment to check on her. Don't worry. I know how to keep a person hidden and cared for."

Something in her face says she's not reassured in the least. "I want to see her. I want to go get her and bring her home."

I meet Adrian's eyes over her shoulder. "Is that wise? She isn't wrapped up in this whole council business. As far as I can tell, the world has forgotten she even exists. Wouldn't it be better if we kept it that way rather than put her in the council's crosshairs too?"

Valentina looks as if she wants to argue, but after a moment, she drops her chin and shakes her head. "Maybe you're right. We should keep her safe and protected until all of this blows over, and then we can bring her home like she deserves."

Adrian rubs her arms to comfort her.

A tiny part of me envies that comfort, the soft touch of human connection meant to heal, not harm. I seem to only ever get hurt.

She spins in his embrace and wraps her arms around his neck. I give them this moment even as I'm mentally rushing them to get me the hell out of here.

When Adrian releases her, she faces me again. "The live stream you did set some of our more avid supporters on edge. They are demanding a recall of the council, and you be put on a sort of bail until you can be retried for your—the crimes. We are taking you home with us."

I surge to my feet and keep my hands low so she doesn't see anything Adrian might kill me for later. Her eyes rove up to the ceiling once she realizes I'm only in my underwear. "They kept you like this?"

"It doesn't matter." I rush toward the door. "Let's go before they change their mind and lock us all in."

Adrian pounds on the cell door, and it swings open to reveal a guard. Fatty, I'd say, by the look of him.

The guard steps out of the way, and Adrian invades his space. "Clothes. Now. I'm not taking him outside like this."

A voice cuts in from the end of the hall. "Oh, but he looks so nice this way. I decided to make it his uniform."

A cold chill cascades down my spine, and I squeeze my eyes shut. I'd hoped she wouldn't come, but why wouldn't she when she can rub my face in her deeds.

She steps closer and runs her hand down my arm. "We had so much fun together, but it looks like you get to leave for a bit. Don't worry, I'll see you again soon."

I'm about one second from grabbing her and slamming her face into the wall when Valentina slaps her hand off me with a sneer. "Don't worry, I'll be seeing you again soon too."

## 2

## ROSE

Is it Wednesday? I study the calendar on the wall from the big black X over the last date that Kai showed up here. The same time every week, but now it's past the new X on the calendar and he didn't come. No one did except the cleaning lady, Parker, who is due on the red X days. Today is a red X day, which means it would be Wednesday.

I scratch my scalp and then gather my dirty hair up into a messy bun. It's long and ridiculous, but there's no one to cut it, so I just wash it when I think about it and leave it up the rest of the time.

It's not like there's anyone to see me or notice the fact that my blonde hair, once stained red from my own blood for weeks, isn't clean or styled properly. Hell, I basically live in the oversized sweats Kai gave me when he brought me here months ago. They smelled like him before. Now, not so much.

I stare at the red X again and check the clock on the small stove. The green numbers seem to stare back at me. Okay, maybe it's time to take my meds.

The box is on the counter. For weeks, Kai had to portion them out for me one at a time, but now, I do it myself. If anything, it gives me something to do. While I'm glad for my safety and the care Kai gives to my health, I'm so fucking bored.

Of course, there's a big-screen TV in the living room and one entire room jam-packed with books, but that doesn't mean I don't get tired of being alone. Though the thought of seeing other people makes my fingers go numb, and panic grips my chest tight.

I stare at the little entryway that leads to the door as if I continue to face off with it, maybe someone will magically show up and whisk me away. New surroundings might be nice—no people but a different space. Something new to look at. Even on the days Kai shows up, I get nervous and sweaty and cannot think or speak straight. Tongue-tied by a man. How far I've fallen in a few short months.

A few short months that feel like years and years. I feel so much older than my twenty-three years. I guess an attempted murder will do that to a girl.

I flip the top of the pill sorter with a pop and scoop out a quarter's worth of various pharmaceuticals. Kai always fills my prescriptions for me, so I don't know if any of this is even legal. I suppose with him, it doesn't matter.

I grab the water bottle near the sink and swig back the pills, taking a big gulp to get them all down. Then I rinse the rancid plastic aftertaste and replace the water bottle.

Yeah…still fucking bored.

I'm sure Parker will be here soon, but she refuses to speak to me. The rare occasion she talks to me is only to ask my preference for cleaning or laundry. All topics I have zero opinion on. Not anymore, at least.

The lock rattles on the door, and keys clatter against the solid steel. I freeze. My heart ping pongs up my throat, sticking tight.

Parker comes in and resets the long line of high-end locks down the door. It takes me a second to slowly unclench my muscles, relaxing inch by inch as my online therapist has walked me through over and over.

Parker is a small woman. She must be in her forties, but her black hair has only a few streaks of gray. She's short, but most women are compared to my five-foot-eight height. Shorter even than my cousin, Valentina, who is tiny. She gives me a quick nod, sets the bag of groceries on the counter, and heads toward the bedrooms in the back. She always starts back to front, working her way toward the door when she cleans.

I slide off the wooden stool and start unpacking the groceries. It's the least I can do since she keeps me from having to scrub my own toilet.

Since I'm the only person who lives here, the groceries are minimal. Just enough to get me from today until Parker returns the following week. Some produce, noodles, and simple basics I can cook or eat raw, depending on my mood.

After I fold up her reusable tote and place it by the door for her to take home, it occurs to me she might know why Kai didn't come to the apartment this week. He is her boss, but then again, I'm his…I don't know what, really…so someone should have said something to me anyway. Changes in the routine make me nervous and twitchy. Two new sides of me have emerged since my attack. Two new sides of myself that I hate.

It takes me a second to rally my courage and head around the corner to find Parker. She's throwing my laundry in the washer when I spot her and hover nearby. She acknowledges me with a quick flick of her eye but says nothing to encourage me to come closer.

"Um…Parker…excuse me," I try.

She drops her hands and stares at me head-on. Hard enough it makes me want to take a step back and retreat from the intensity of her gaze. "Yes, Miss Smith."

Of course, she thinks my name is Jane Smith. You'd think someone as smart as Kai would come up with a better cover name. But I doubt Parker needs anything more involved since she doesn't use my name more than once a month.

According to a passing comment from Parker when she first started cleaning here, Kai is Mr. Smith, my brother. "Have you heard from Mr. Smith recently?"

Her honey-brown eyes narrow on me. "Mr. Smith? No, only for payment and grocery lists. Nothing more."

She turns back to the laundry like that's the end of the discussion, but it wasn't much of an answer at all. It tells me absolutely nothing. And I'm getting so tired of people telling me nothing.

I follow her, stomping my feet, feeling childish. It doesn't matter, though, because no one is here to witness this except her, and she's made it very clear that she won't be engaging me in a fight.

She starts making the bed as if I haven't stormed around her and now stand on the other side of the bed, glaring her way. "Excuse me…" I try.

As I expect, she ignores me. It's fine. She usually does, so I've stopped trying to engage her, but Kai has never failed to show up before either, so maybe we all need to let our little oddities fly out the window.

"Excuse me," I prompt again.

This time, she gives me a little glare of her own, pressing her thin mouth into a line. "Yes, Miss Smith? Can I help you with something?"

I roll my eyes, wanting to shake her. Does she know my name isn't really Smith? I mean, does she care as long as she's getting a regular paycheck? Does she know what kind of man Kai is? On that note, do I? I've been locked in this apartment for months and months. Kai comes and goes, and we speak briefly when he does, but we've never had a long conversation, never sat down to discuss the future. I can't stay here forever, nor do I want to.

"Yes, I want to know if you've heard from Mr. Smith at all. It's very urgent that I speak to him, and I don't have a way to do that here in the apartment."

This statement earns me another glare. Like I'm saying more than she wants to hear. Saying more than she wants to know. "I'm not sure what you mean, Miss Smith. I only hear from Mr. Smith when he needs to send me anything special for the grocery list. Otherwise, he sends me my paycheck every week, and that's the extent of our conversations. I'm afraid I can't help you."

She shakes the sheet out hard enough that the edge almost clips me. As if it's the punctuation to the end of our conversation.

I storm back out to the living room to look at the calendar one more time. Maybe I'm confused. It wouldn't be the first time. And me being confused is far better than the routine being messed up or thinking that maybe Kai is never coming back and I'll be stuck here for the rest of my life. Gently, I trail my finger over the red X like it might bite me if I press too hard. I'm definitely not confused. He should have already been here.

Instead of chasing Parker again, I take my usual seat on the stool at the countertop bar. I grab one of the apples from the bowl I just filled up, slide off the stool, rinse it, then return. While I chew, I consider what I'll do if Kai doesn't show up for another week. That would certainly mean he's given up on me. Or what if something happened to him? That thought hadn't crossed my mind because he always seems so…in control. But now that I think about it, what if he's dead? Then no one will pay Parker, and I'll be left here with no food and no way out.

I feel the beginnings of an anxiety spiral, as my therapist calls them, and start counting sensations to try to bring myself out. The crunch of the apple in my mouth, the taste of it. The grounding of my feet on the rungs of the stool. The cool air from the overhead fan on my shoulders. Tears stream down my cheeks now, but I dash them away. It was enough to pull me out, and I finish my apple and toss the core in the trash can under the sink.

God, why am I like this? Every time I let myself get too deep into my feelings, I spiral into a panic attack. No matter what the feelings are. Basically, the only time I can feel something without panicking is when I binge-watch soap operas on the TV and let myself cry it out. Hilary wasn't supposed to die, yet…no panic attack then, just tears, a pile of tissues, and the cozy warm blanket I keep on the back of the small loveseat.

I creep up on the thought again … what if Kai is hurt? What if he needs help? I don't have a way to contact anyone. He gave me a burner phone ages ago, but it's a flip phone and only has his number programmed inside. Not to mention, it's dead at the bottom of my nightstand. He specified that it can only be used in an emergency, and asking him if he's okay doesn't seem to align with his definition of an emergency.

At the very least, maybe I should plug that phone in just in case he needs to contact me. What if he already tried, and I've been sitting here worried for no reason?

I race into the bedroom, thankful Parker has already changed the bedding, and moved on to the bathroom. It takes me a minute to find the phone wedged under a couple of books. I hunt down the plug next and smile when it dings obnoxiously to let me know it's turning on.

Once the little light comes on, I flip the silver phone open and stare at the screen. No messages.

Well, shit.

I hear Parker shuffle out of the bathroom and back into the kitchen. What if she's my only chance at getting out of here? What if Kai isn't returning, and I'll need to escape on my own?

I rush out to the kitchen, and she stares at me warily while she gathers the trash and her purse.

"Wait, Parker, please. Take me with you."

Just as I finish speaking, Kai steps around the entrance to the kitchen, his keys in his hand, leveling me with a look that chills my bones.

## 3

## KAI

*P*arker casts a worried glance back and forth between Rose and me, but I give her a megawatt smile. It doesn't reach my eyes because I just don't have the energy in me today to make it, but the woman doesn't seem to notice.

I fish the envelope out of my suit jacket and hand it to her. It's fat, stuffed full of cash. "Take this. We won't be needing your services anymore."

Her eyes go wide. "Mr. Smith, I wasn't going to take her anywhere, I swear."

I try to sound reassuring, hoping I'm hitting the mark. "No, it's not you, Parker. Miss Smith and I are going on a vacation of sorts. When we return, I'll contact you to resume your services. But I didn't want to leave you without income while we were away. So take this money, and you should be all set for a while." I have no intention of bringing her back here, but she doesn't need to know that. This is more cash than she's probably seen at once in her lifetime, so she won't ask questions, and that's what I'm paying for.

She hikes her purse up her shoulder and gives me a nod. I watch her leave and then lock the door behind her.

Rose is still at the counter with her arms wrapped around herself. "You didn't come last week. I thought something might have happened to you. That's the only reason I asked her to take me with her."

I scan her head to toe, from the sweats she's cuffed at her ankles and wrists to the messy bun on top of her head. "When did you last take a shower?"

She stiffens. "Yesterday."

"And when did you last wash your hair?"

This time, she throws her chin up. "Why do you care if my hair is clean or dirty? You don't live here."

What she doesn't know is that I come here more often than she thinks. She just spends a lot of time in her own bedroom that she barely notices when I check the camera and sneak into the room on the far side of the apartment that I keep locked. When I left Rose that first time, I made sure she understood it was off-limits, and Parker knew as well. No one goes into my room without permission, and that's how I like to keep it. As far as I can tell, she hasn't tried, at least according to the security cameras I have installed that cover every inch of this place.

I sigh and throw my jacket over the back of the loveseat. "I'm tired. I'm going to go grab a shower really fast, and then we need to talk."

"What you said about a vacation, is that true? Are we leaving here, or did you lie to get her to go away?"

I don't bother looking back as I unlock my room and step through the door. "I lied. I won't be calling her again."

It's cruel of me to leave her with questions like that, but I don't have it in me to explain myself right now. Adrian is the only person who doesn't make me explain myself after almost every statement. Everyone else usually requires some explanation or direction. For once in my life, I'd love to meet someone who can figure things out and work them out in their own mind so I don't have to break them down. It gets exhausting.

I strip off my clothes and throw them into a pile in the bathroom. Right now, all I want is the stench of that council bitch off my body. Even now, I can smell the scent of her perfume and cunt. I gag hard and clamp my hand over my mouth to avoid vomiting. She's not here, but I won't give her the satisfaction.

I turn the water as hot as it will go and step under the spray. It blasts down onto my shoulders, easing some of the tension I'd built there over my last week in lockup. It only takes me a few minutes to scrub myself down, but I do it twice and test the air to make sure all I smell is the soft scent of my soap. The clothes I'd rather burn than wear again, even if the suit cost a small fortune. Money is money. There's always more to be found when it's needed.

The bathroom is fogged when I step out and turn off the water. I brush my teeth and shave quickly too. I'm not sure how long we'll be traveling, and I might not get another chance for a couple of days.

After I finish, I walk through the adjoining closet and find the clothes I want to wear. Not my usual suit, but a cashmere sweater, slacks, and dress shoes. Extremely casual for me but comfortable enough to travel in for a few days. Besides, no one usually sees me out of my suits. If the council is watching for me, they might overlook me if I'm wearing different attire.

I take the clothing to the bedroom and stop short with the hangers dangling from my fingers. Rose is sitting cross-legged on my bed.

I swallow hard, praying she hasn't been sitting there long. If her scent has been imprinted on the bedding, I'll never be able to get to sleep. "What the fuck are you doing in here?"

Her mouth hangs open as she stares at my bare chest, the towel tucked low around my hips. I dried off, but my short hair is still wet enough to send water drops down my body. Her eyes fixate on one droplet, and she tracks its progress from my collarbone to disappear into the edge of my towel. It's more eye contact than I've gotten in the months she's been in my care.

I snap my fingers. "Eyes up here. What are you doing in here?"

She shakes herself, and a flush crawls up her neck and into her cheeks, staining her face a bright pink. "You said…you said we were going somewhere. Are we leaving?"

I toss my clothing on the bed right next to her, making her jump. "We are leaving, but I'm not ready to discuss it until I've planned out the details. Besides, I need a nap first. I've been up for what feels like days."

"Days?" she echoes. "Why?"

I pin her with a look. "It's none of your business. Now please, go away so I can get some rest."

Carefully, I strip the undershirt off the hanger and gently unfold the sweater. A hand clamps my bicep, and I react before I think.

When I blink again, Rose is on the other side of the room, clutching her arm to her chest with a fine sheen of tears coating her eyes.

Fuck. Fucking. Fuck.

"Rose…"

She dashes out the door, slamming it on her way out. I'm more tense than I thought if I shoved her away before realizing who touched me. And more tired since I know she's the only one in the room with me. All I hear is that bitch's laughter in my ears and her panting. It's taking everything I have left to shut it all out enough to function.

I stare at the door. No. I need to make sure I didn't break something or hurt her too badly. At the very least to ensure we can travel sooner rather than later.

She's hiding in her room, as usual. I open the door and skirt the bed to find her on the floor on the other side. "What are you doing?"

She is clutching her wrist tightly in her other hand.

I crouch beside her, the towel splitting over my knee. She stares at my bare skin for a heartbeat, her face going redder, and then she glances away, refusing to answer.

"Let me see so I can make sure nothing is broken."

With a huff, she shoves her arm at me. "You aren't Superman or anything. I'm fine. I've had way worse than this."

The tension stretches tight between us as if we both remember exactly how bad she's had it. Her eyes glaze over as she stares off, and I drop her arm to catch her face in my hands. Without any struggle at all, she lets me cup her cheeks and jaw, but I don't want her submission. I want her to fight for her freedom. That's the woman I can see in her eyes. That's the woman I want to do battle with.

I trace my thumbs along her jawline until they meet at her chin, anchoring my fingers behind her head. Then I ever so gently tilt her face back so I meet her eyes head-on. "Look at me, Rose."

Her breath fans against my mouth, and she comes back to herself, blinking away the haze. "What?"

"You were saying I'm not strong enough to hurt you. I could crush you so easily, but I'm not a man who likes to hurt women. It's so much more fun when they fight me on an even playing field."

She blinks again and jerks from my hold. "You're so weird. My arm is fine, so you should probably get dressed."

I lick my lips and shake my head, the scent of her body clinging to me. Soap. Just the soft scent of lavender soap wafting off her body. I draw the scent into my lungs and shift up to standing. "Pack your things and get dressed in clothes you don't mind wearing outside."

She scrambles off the floor to face me. "I don't want to go outside."

"You were ready to race off with Parker, so it shouldn't be a problem, right?"

A little line grows in the middle of her forehead while she worries her bottom lip between her teeth. Then lets it pop out. "But that was because I thought I'd be trapped here forever if you had run off and died somewhere."

I shake my head with my hands on my hips. "I'm not arguing about this right now. I need to pack too and get a little sleep before we can leave. I suggest you do the same."

Heading back to my room to get dressed, I whip off the towel once I clear my door and hear the lock mechanism catch the strike plate. What I don't expect is her to come barreling in after me, only to skid to a stop on the hardwood when she catches sight of me. "Oh, my god, you're naked."

A part of me wants to snatch up the towel and cover myself. That long-buried part of me that had been so recently violated. Another part of me wants her to see it all. The little whisper in the back of my mind that I've been studiously ignoring for months. "Yes, you did just shove into my room."

"I'm…well…you…" She waves at me, rolling her eyes up to the ceiling. "We weren't done discussing this."

I grab my underwear off the bed and slip them on. "I was done discussing it, as evident by me leaving your room, coming in mine, and closing the door."

She clears her throat loudly, twisting her hands into her oversized sweatshirt. "I don't want to go out there. I'm..." She gulps so loudly that I hear it from a couple of feet away. "I'm scared."

Shit. Things had been going well with her therapist, so I assumed she'd be ready when the time came to leave this apartment. This is my safe house, the place I always come back to. She can't stay here forever, and I never planned to let her. "There's nothing to be afraid of."

A fine tremor rolls through her, and she looks like she might cry. I step up and cradle her face again, tilting her to look me in the eyes once more. "I will keep you safe. No one will touch you without your permission. If they do, I'll kill them."

She sucks in a breath. "You will?"

I nod slowly. "Do you believe me?"

Another thick gulp. "Shouldn't it scare me when you say that?"

Carefully, I shrug. "Maybe, but if it doesn't, then don't worry about it."

Her eyes go liquid again, a sheen of tears coating them. "But I should be scared. I should be."

Without another word, she races out of the room, and I hope it's to pack because, if not, I'm taking her as is, and she'll have to survive.

It's time for both of us to disappear.

# 4
## ROSE

*H*e brought me new clothes. It's the first thought that sits in my head when I snap awake in the morning. The nightmares dragged me under for too long, and blessedly when I woke, I couldn't remember the shadows clinging to my mind like cobwebs. It's a small mercy that at least some of what happened to me is a complete blank. I remember way more than I wanted to as it stood.

The clothes hang in the closet—pressed, clean, and ready for someone who isn't me. I'm not the girl who dresses up anymore, the one who likes to make clothes and dreams of fancy parties. These days, my dreams revolve around soap opera reruns and hoping Parker brought a new paperback from the grocery store with my order. Those clothes—the pressed slacks and the rich silk of the shirts—belong to someone else and not to this version of me.

The alarm on the bedside table blares loudly, and I flip it off. Kai must have snuck into my room and set it after I fell asleep. The asshole. My door had been locked, but of course, he has keys to anything and everything. A liberty he doesn't extend to me.

Once the ringing in my ears stops, I throw back the covers and stand, glaring at the clothing as I enter the bathroom and angrily brush my teeth. If I don't get ready, I don't have any illusions that he will come in here and drag me out as is. I have to leave this house today, so I'll try to make it on my terms. Or, at the very least, give myself the illusion of choice.

When I finish brushing my teeth, I do the same for my hair, then take the fastest shower I can and hop back out. He's never walked in on me before, but he's also never spent the night here before that I know of. I refuse to let him catch me unawares. I quickly braid my hair, slap on some moisturizer, and go back into the bedroom to have a stare-down with the wardrobe.

Wearing these clothes would make me feel like a fraud. I slip into some plain cotton underwear that's soft, comfortable, and easy. This silk and wool do not scream soft, comfortable, or easy. The black on black will complement my skin tone, but hell, wearing them feels a little too much like giving in to him. Something I'm determined not to do.

Instead of donning the clothes, I grab the worn-in fluffy robe I love off the bathroom door and slip it on. At the very least, I can give myself a little more time in comfort until he orders me into that...costume.

I open the door an inch and peer out into the kitchen. A light glows softly from the other end, so he must be awake. His voice, deep and dark, reaches me, but I have to focus on the words because his tone is too low to make out from this distance.

After a moment of craning my neck, keeping my ear at the opening, I catch the word Valentina and freeze, my fingers gripping the wood of the door so tight they ache.

Valentina.

When I'd mostly recovered, I'd only learned that she also survived the attack, but he refuses to give me anything else. Then the next time I asked about her, Kai backed me into the wall and told me not to ask again. That he'd make sure I never got to see her if I did. It was the only time I allowed myself to cry in front of him, begging him to let me go to her, but he refused, saying being near her would put everyone in danger. At the time, I hadn't been able to tell if he thought I was a danger to her or if he meant something else. He hadn't budged on his position, and I stopped asking to see my cousin, hoping, one day, maybe she'd come and see me. So far, she has not.

I shove down the old wave of sadness, gathering it all up with the rest of the emotions I refuse to let myself feel, and creep out of the bedroom, moving carefully, praying he's in his room, and I can eat breakfast in peace.

Of course, I don't have that kind of luck, and I know it. He sits at the countertop bar, the dim overhead light bouncing off the shiny surface of his hair, like it's still wet from his shower.

I self-consciously run my hand over my braid and toss it behind my shoulder. There isn't anything to feel self-conscious about. I've showered and put on clean clothes today. My soft worn-out robe doesn't compare to the elegant lines of his ridiculously fitted suit, but I'm not the one who decided to leave this place. That's all him, and right now, I'm petty enough to force him to deal with the consequences of that choice.

Instead of acknowledging him, I walk right by the counter and grab a bowl from the dish drainer. I can feel his eyes on me as I pour my fruit cereal into the bowl and smother it in milk.

He'd stopped talking when I came out, and I carry my bowl to the counter just in time for him to end the call and slip his phone into his suit jacket. I duck my chin and ignore him harder, plunging a spoon into my cereal to eat quickly and loudly. Maybe I can scare him off to his own room and be left in peace for a little while.

Nope. Again, no luck. "You're not dressed."

I finish swallowing and decide not answering might be too childish. "I'm wearing a robe. I'm dressed."

He huffs, the noise calling me the child I feel like right now. Yet around him, I can't help but push. "You know what I mean. I left you some clothes. Hurry up and eat, then change, so we can leave."

I dunk my spoon in the bowl and glare at him. This earns me a glare in return, and he snakes his hand out to steal my bowl in a move so fast I don't have time to react. "Hey!"

"Stop acting like a petulant child. Eat your food, change, then we are leaving. All I want to hear out of you is okay."

I only glare.

"A nod will also suffice."

Finally, I nod, and he eases my bowl toward me. I snatch it back and shovel the food down, then drink the sugary milk to chase it. Since Parker won't be back, I wash the bowl and spoon myself, then spin to brace my hips on the counter.

"I can't wear those clothes. They will be too tight, uncomfortable."

He scans something on his phone, reading faster than I can, even on a good day. "I didn't ask you to be comfortable. I only asked you to be presentable."

"Why?"

This time when his eyes clash with mine, there's an angry spark there. A challenge. "Now is not the time for questions. We have to leave, and we have to do it in the next hour, so if you aren't dressed by then, I'm going to peel that robe off you and let you walk out of here naked."

I clear my throat. "I'm not naked. I'm wearing underwear."

His eyes shutter as he scans what he can see of my body, neck to knees. "Fine, in your underwear then. Do you really want everyone out there to see you mostly naked?"

I draw the robe around me tighter as if it can shield me from his gaze. To be honest, the thought of anyone seeing my scars—the ones Sal gave me during that last attack and some of the ones before—makes my stomach roil. The breakfast I just ate sits differently now as if it might come up at any moment. I gaze off, a flashback hitting me hard until a voice draws me back.

Kai is there, standing so close to me I can see the black flecks in his irises. His eyes look one color from far away, but standing here so close, I can see they aren't. He's got my robe open, his hands on my waist, skin on skin, like a baby needing the contact to thrive. "Are you back with me?"

I gulp hard and nod, barely aware as he pulls his big warm fingers away from my body. It's nothing he hasn't seen before after months of caring for my injuries, but now that I'm healed, it's as if he's found every reason not to touch me unless it's necessary.

He clears his throat and steps back. "All that white cotton is charming, but I doubt you want the entire world to see it. Go change, Rose, before I change my mind and drag you out of here just as you are."

"Why do I have to wear that? It makes me feel like a fraud."

He bends his knees to duck to my level, a trick to meet my eyes head-on. "Why? This was your life before. You had fine clothes, right?

I shrug. "Only for when we went out in public where people might see. I usually made everything I wore out of scraps from old outfits either me or Val had outgrown."

He flinches at the mention of Val but doesn't say anything else. "Just go change and stop arguing with me for once. I will strip this robe from your body and put the clothes on you myself if you don't do it quickly."

Since he's not a man who makes idle threats, I don't wait for him to tell me again. I scurry back to my room and close the door.

My exhale escapes harsh and loud in the empty room. My skin is crawling from him touching me, his clean almond scent still clinging to my robe in places. I don't like being touched anymore, yet when his hands met my skin, it wasn't the revulsion I usually feel from the touch of another but something else. Something that scared me far more.

I stare at the clothes, then drag them down and put them on, cursing Kai every second. As usual, it all fits me perfectly, as if he's tailored the fabric himself just for me. The silk of the black shirt is soft against my skin, lying flat and straight against my body. I tuck the shirt into the slacks and grab the leather ballet flats on the floor near my dresser.

When I come out of the bedroom, he gives me a quick once-over and then focuses on his phone. "Come sit. We'll be leaving in just a second."

I swallow, not wanting to sit so close to him while things are rolling around inside me unsettled. But I also don't want to argue more and get him in a worse mood. Not so early in the day when I don't know how long we'll be stuck together.

"Can I ask where we are going?" I manage, sitting on the stool next to him.

He answers, but I blink, and it's like I missed something. "I'm sorry, I didn't catch that."

This time, he turns to face me and tucks his phone into his pocket again. "I said the plane is ready. We can leave in a moment."

I nod. Things seem to be slowing down, and my body, which had been coiled tight since I woke up, is relaxing. "What are we waiting for then?"

He reaches out and wraps his hands around my waist gently. "For the drugs I slipped into your cereal to kick in. Don't worry, it's just a little Xanax to keep you calm until we reach our destination."

"You motherfu—"

Darkness swallows me whole, and it wears Kai's face.

# 5

## KAI

It occurs to me that I should feel bad about drugging her. Or at least not giving her the choice of medicating for the flight. However, knowing how she feels about going outside and how much of a battle it had already turned out to be just to get her to pack and come with me, I opt for ease rather than her autonomy. A decision I'm sure I'll hear about the moment she wakes up.

I sit back on the plush leather couch and sigh, the sound of the high crackling fire to my left lulling me into calm I rarely manage these days. If I weren't afraid she'd wake scared and alone, I'd take a little nap myself, but I don't trust her to be calm when it's time, and I won't leave her to her fear like so many before me.

Snow is falling in a steady blanket outside. Inches have already accumulated since we landed and took the SUV up the mountain alone. Not that she noticed anything in her deep slumber. The bags still sit by the door, but it's something we can deal with later, once she's awake and no longer cursing my existence.

Valentina told me to take Rose somewhere safe and hide. Adrian agreed, and that's all the direction I needed to get out of the city for a while. At the very least, I won't have to see a single council member out here. Maybe they will forget about me with the new season starting soon. Or maybe I'll get tired of waiting and make a move on them myself. Death is better than uncertainty.

When we arrived a few hours ago, I placed her on the long couch directly across from the fireplace so I could keep an eye on her. The second she starts stirring, I ease out of the chair to her side and kneel next to her shoulders. "Rose, can you hear me? Wake up."

She moves a bit more and then blinks her eyes open only to let out a huff and squeeze them shut again. "What...how? Why is it so bright? Why does my mouth feel like I swallowed a handful of cotton balls?"

I shove off the couch to stand and grab her a glass of water from a pitcher on the counter. When I return, I gently help her sit and then gingerly sit beside her, so I don't jostle her too much. Maybe I gave her too high of a dose, but the doctor assured me it would be enough to keep her sedated without any ill effects. Slowly, I wrap her hands around the glass of water and help her bring it to her lips. She guzzles it down greedily, letting it dribble down her chin until the glass is empty.

"Do you want more?"

She shakes her head, blinking her eyes open once more. "No, thank you. That was enough."

I set the glass on the long wood coffee table and study her face. She's barely squinting her eyes open, and her mouth is twisted in her usual scowl. Her hair is mussed, the braid piecemeal after all the travel and then her fitful sleep. "What's going on? Why is it so bright in here right now?"

Instead of answering, I shift off the couch to find the remote for the built-in window shades. Her eyes follow me, and when I start the shade, she screeches, "Wait!"

I hit the button to stop it and watch her struggle to stand. Okay, the dose had definitely been too large for her. Maybe it's because she's lost so much weight since the last time the doctor took her vitals. My new mission is to help her put some of it back on. Not that she's too thin, but I liked her curves before, at least what I allowed myself to see. Not much with her being so injured for so long.

"Is that...is that snow?" She carefully makes her way across the room to the huge bank of windows framed by the aged wood beams. "Why is there snow outside?"

"We are on a mountain, and I think that's a blizzard."

She presses her forehead against the glass, her fingers coming up along her cheek to touch the window too. "I've never seen snow like this before. A few inches here or there and some flurries, but nothing like this. There has to be a few feet of it out there right now." Her voice is almost in awe as she stares across the empty white expanse behind the house.

A few hundred feet beyond is a sheer drop-off with an incredible view, but it's impossible to see with the snow cover. I toss the remote on the couch and join her at the window. "The weather predicts another couple of feet by the time the blizzard passes in a few days."

"Where are we?"

I clear my throat, not wanting to lie, so I give her the best answer I can. "In another city, in the mountains, we are safe."

Her eyes go round, her face a little pale. "Were we not before? Safe, I mean?"

I remember I didn't explain why I'd been away or about any of the trouble with the council. It's not a quick story to sum up, but I try to be brief. "It's complicated, but I got on the council's radar, and Adrian suggested we get out of town for a while, at least until everything blows over."

Her eyes scan my features as if she's searching for the truth between the barest explanation I've provided. "Are we safe here?"

I nod. "No one knows about this place. The property belongs to my family. No one ever uses it, so we can stay here as long as we need to."

The awestruck look enters her eyes again, and she turns to watch the snow. "It's so beautiful."

To be honest, I'm surprised she's being so reasonable about all of this. Maybe it's the medication talking, or perhaps, she needs a change of scenery just as bad as I do. "Do you want to see the house?"

I wave behind her, and she spins to face the living room. Her gaze rakes over the wood beams, the kitchen to the right, the upper level with the bedrooms, and then the other rooms off the lower level. "Okay."

It takes a moment to shift around the furniture, and I lead her to the bathroom on the main floor, give the kitchen a vague wave, and then show her the way to the garage where both the vehicles and the weapons are stored. When I show her how to get to the weapons, something closes off in her face. "If I have to fight anyone, we are probably already dead."

Her statement sparks hot anger in my chest. "That's not acceptable. We don't give up, no matter what. Am I clear?"

Something darker enters her eyes. A knowledge I wish so dearly she hadn't been burdened with. The scent of her lavender soap wafts around me as she eases past to go back into the house without a word. Instead of arguing, I grab her bag by the door and show her the bedroom. It's a suite with a balcony, giving even more amazing mountain views. The bathroom has an in-ground tub and a waterfall shower, but she barely notices because she's still mesmerized by the snow.

It could be so easy like this. If we stay here, no one will find us, and we could both spend the rest of our lives in peace.

Needing to peel my mind away from the idea, I step up beside her and stare out at the snowy mountains. "We are here all alone, so we'll be responsible for our own cooking and cleaning."

She nods, not looking at me. "That's fine. I don't mind cooking or cleaning for myself."

It's on the tip of my tongue to tease her about her apartment—our apartment—but maybe she's right. I never gave her the chance to cook or clean for herself while she was there. From day one, she's had a keeper from the doctors to Parker.

"I'm not great at cooking myself, but I'll do my best." I'm not sure why I say it. She doesn't care if I can cook, and saying I'm unable to sounds a little too close to admitting weakness for me.

A lock of her hair falls down to graze the side of her neck. Before I think about it, I reach and sweep it behind her ear. She flinches hard, almost falling forward against the window with the effect.

With my hand still hovering in the air between us, I study her profile. No longer is she relaxed. Her entire body is coiled tight as if she's waiting for me to strike out at her. An ache in my chest builds until I have to step away. Even if she thought I'd hit her, all she did was brace for it and wait to take the blow. She didn't slap my hand away, or leave, or move, none of it.

I swallow hard, bile building in my throat. "I'll be downstairs if you need anything," I manage and slip out the door before I say something that will truly anger her. Or shake her awake so I can see the spark in her eyes enough that she shoves me or hits me back. Anything but the woman standing there waiting for me to vent my anger on her body. Not when I've never given her a reason to think of me as that kind of man.

Needing something to do, I slip on one of the oversized coats hanging by the door, change my dress shoes for boots, drop my suit jacket, and go outside to find the woodpile. I stay there, splitting wood with an axe until a small pile grows beside the chopping stump.

After a while, I strip off my jacket, yank on my loosened tie, and unbutton my dress shirt to pull it out of my pants. Any other day, I can face down an enemy, fight, and do whatever needs doing in my typical uniform, but right now, it feels constricting, like the expensive fabric is cutting off circulation to places I desperately need blood and oxygen.

My heartbeat sounds loud in my ears, and my hands ache from the tight grip of the axe. I've used the manual labor to focus my anger away until it becomes more, sapping me of the anger and my energy at the same time.

I'm tired. So tired of the fighting and the violence. Of people assuming I'm the monster waiting in the dark to take them. All at Adrian's bidding, of course.

I shove the thoughts away and gather the wood in a snow-crusted basket to carry inside.

The heat hits me first, and then the scent of soup. Something spicy. I try to single out the smells, and underneath the heat of the spices, I catch the scent of biscuits baking. She's been just as busy while I've been outside working. It takes a moment to load the wood up and then hang up my coat. Once I wash my hands, face, and change into something more comfortable, I join her in the kitchen, keeping my distance.

She's working quietly, not a sound in the house except the snow outside battering against the windows. "I didn't know you could cook."

There's a moment in the silence, heavy, holding its breath. She takes so long to answer that I don't think she's going to. "You don't know anything about me. Yet you've always pictured this spoiled princess incapable of doing things on her own. I'm not the one who hired Parker. You did."

I nod, giving her that one. She's right. All I know is the barest glimpse of what my spies reported and the tiniest threads I'd picked up in passing from Valentina. "So tell me then. What do I need to know about you?"

## 6

## ROSE

The snow falls through the night and into the morning. I repeatedly woke overnight and settled myself back to sleep, somehow feeling safer than I'd ever felt before. As if the snow could blanket my sins, my past, my pain. I glance at the clock, checking the time, trying to decide if I should go down to grab food or if I'll run into Kai or not. It's not that I want to avoid him, just that I'd rather not see him and have everything come crashing back down around my shoulders. He's a stark reminder of what I've been through. A perpetual trigger.

Peeling myself off the floor in front of the window, I huddle in the blanket I'd stolen from the bed and check the hallway. The coast seems clear, the lower level dark and silent.

I creep out into the hall, keeping watch, using the blanket to cover my bare legs, panties, and plain T-shirt I'd been sleeping in. It should be all right. I only want to grab something to eat and scurry back up to my room.

When I reach the kitchen, a slight whooshing sound filters in. Could it be the snow falling off the roof? I crane my neck, trying to catch the location, then creep out of the kitchen to another hallway. The second I find the source of the noise, I freeze. Kai is on the ground doing push-ups in barely-there shorts and no shirt. The music from his earbuds is so loud I can hear it blasting from the doorway. He's facing the opposite wall, so I have the perfect view of the slope of his back.

Since he seems to be in his own little world, I leave him to it, heading back to the kitchen. I don't make it more than a few steps before something snags my blanket, dragging it off my shoulders, and I'm pressed belly first into the icy wall.

I assess in stages. The hard hot body along my back, the bare skin of his muscular thighs on my ass, then the iron grip of the hands around my wrists, keeping me pinned to the wall.

Panic rises in my chest. A wave of it threatens to choke me, forcing me to gag on empty air.

"Shhhh..." a voice whispers in my ear. Just like that, I'm back in the dark, another man against me, another man holding me down, another man whispering to be quiet.

My entire body trembles in his hold so violently he has to release some of the tension on my wrists. The opportunity is the only option. I snap my hand out of his grip and slam my fist back into the side of his face.

He hisses out a breath and then recaptures my hand easily, pinning me even tighter now so that I feel every curve of his body against my back. "Be quiet. I thought I heard something."

I'm still trembling, my nerves vibrating, every part of me poised to run the second I can get free, but I'm quiet. As if some part of my mind knows he won't hurt me, not deliberately. Not maliciously.

"Do you hear that?" He breathes against my ear. It shoots another round of shivers through my body, and inside, I roil at both the pleasure and the terror in it.

"I can't hear anything right now," I grit out, hoping he doesn't make me explain that the sound of my heart blasting in my ears is all I can manage.

"Breathe and focus," he whispers. "Listen."

I try to wiggle out from his hold again, but it just makes him press me tighter, lining our bodies up more as he squats a bit to align our curves. I'm seconds away from screaming, not because of him, but from all the skin-on-skin contact. He's slightly sweaty wherever he touches me, and some deep part of me wants to lick the salt from his skin just for a second to see what he tastes like.

Another wave of nausea rolls through me, and the shaking starts again.

His hands ease ever so softly off mine, and I twist them down to tuck them against my chest. "Easy, easy," he whispers like I'm some feral animal ready to snap at the slightest provocation.

"What is it?" I ask, my voice petulant even to myself. "What is so important that you need to accost me and scare the shit out of me?"

He tucks his chin into the crook of my neck, his breath fanning down into my cleavage on full display. "It's my job to keep you safe. If something happens to you, Valentina and Adrian will skin me alive and then put me back on guard duty."

Finally, his words sink in, and a different kind of panic takes hold. "You think someone is out there? For us?"

I stare at the gravelly pattern on the wall, folding my hands, making myself a smaller target. "What do we do?" I whisper.

A soft laugh brushes along my neck, raising goose bumps. "It was probably just an animal, but I'll go change and check it out."

Torn by the idea of both him touching me and leaving me, I flop my mouth open a few times, then clamp it shut again. "What should I do?"

Carefully, he unfolds from around my body, still standing close but staring out the limitless windows for any kind of disturbance. All I see is the endless snowy expanse. But I'm not Kai, and ever since we first met, I've known he sees more than most.

He squints out the windows, his voice as distant as those mountain ranges beyond. "Get dressed, get your breakfast. I'll be back to check on you in a moment."

When he shifts around me, I snatch the blanket and keep my eyes on him until he disappears up the stairs. I assume he's getting dressed, which I should be doing, too.

Once he's out of sight, and I shield my body with the blanket neck to feet, I sneak up the stairs and dart into my own room.

My stomach lets out an angry growl as if it knows I'm not going down again for a while. Next time I grab food, I'll squirrel away some in my room, just in case this happens again. Then there's no reason to leave at all.

I dig through my bag and find the small e-reader I hid away there. Basically, my only form of entertainment. Kai gave it to me when I was recovering, and I've used it so much the sides are worn from my fingertips.

I always assumed I was buying books on his account, but he's mentioned nothing about what I've chosen to read, and I've never asked him for credit to buy them. Maybe it's just another thing between us we don't talk about. There are other moments tying us together in secrets and silence, but I keep them to myself. As far as I can tell, he doesn't mention my nightmares or how I wake up screaming to Valentina, and I hope to keep it that way. One day, when I see her again, I don't want her to see the broken woman I became before the end.

I climb into the soft bedding and wrap all the blankets around me. Leaning against the headboard, I have a clear view out the window of the snow beyond. I can't think of a dreamier spot. If only I had some snacks to go along with it.

I let myself get lost in the book, and when my bedroom door bangs open a little while later, I blink up at Kai in surprise. He's dressed now, thank goodness, but not in the suits I'm used to seeing him in. This time, he's in jeans, a thick gray wool sweater that stretches across his shoulders, and heavy black combat boots.

If he notices me staring, he doesn't mention it. "You doing okay?"

I swallow hard, the flash of his body against mine making my throat dry. "Yeah, fine," I croak out.

He surveys the room, the windows, then me, and gives me a clipped nod. "You didn't get food, did you?"

It's pointless to lie because he always sees through me. "No, I came back up here when you went to get dressed. Did you see anyone outside?"

"No, just deer tracks leading up the side of the cabin. It was probably curious and sniffing around."

I blink, and he's gone, walking out the door, leaving it open. My e-reader clicked off while we were talking, so I hit the button to start it up again. While it loads, I consider how different he looks outside of his usual clothing. Not that I've seen him regularly since he set me up in that apartment, but still.

The book opens, and I hunker down into the covers more and start reading again. But I barely make it a page when Kai returns with a plate of fruit. He sits on the edge of the bed, setting the plate beside him. "You need to eat."

I keep scanning the book, not looking at him. "And if I say I'm not hungry, are you going to force me to eat?"

Out of the corner of my eye, I see him snag some pineapple and pop it into his mouth. "No, but I might eat it all, and then if you decide you want something, you'll have to get it yourself."

I glance up at his face, judging his sincerity. His features are neutral, as if he doesn't care one way or the other. I reach out and take an apple slice, then take a bite. "Thank you. I could have gotten my own food anyway."

"It's nothing, just what was already available in the refrigerator. I'm sure there will be plenty of time for you to wow me with your culinary prowess."

A snort-laugh slips out of me before I fold my lips in to cover it up.

He's smiling, though, as if he can't believe he just heard me snort and laugh at the same time. "Not much of a chef then, I take it?"

"Are you? I bet you're super good at ordering takeout, though, right?"

He waves the phone I didn't notice in his other hand. "I have all the apps. Unfortunately, they aren't going to help us one bit out here. We're on our own."

"Hope you like cereal."

He shrugs, then grabs another piece of fruit and stands. "I like all kinds of things, Rose. You'd know that if you let me in."

I stiffen, my muscles going as tight as my heart. "It's not like you've been knocking on my door trying to play twenty questions every day. In the beginning, sure, because you wanted to know what I knew about

Novak's operation. That was fine by me. You're here to protect me. You don't have to pretend to like me to do that. I'm a job to you and nothing more."

His voice dips low, vibrating along my skin. "When did I say that?"

"You don't have to say it. I'm not an idiot. In what world would someone like you be interested in someone like me? I'm used goods."

I don't even have time to look away before his hand is on my chin, wrenching my face up so he can stare into my eyes. His hand is braced on the bed beside my hip, his upper body almost on top of my knees. I should be scared. My heartbeat goes out of control, but my mind is calm and clear, unlike earlier when he'd caught me.

"Don't you ever fucking talk about yourself like that again. If I hear it, I'll punish you, and I promise, there are punishments I've been saving just for you, Rose."

I swallow hard, unable to speak with his hand still clenched around my jaw.

He stares into my eyes a second longer, then shoves off the bed, pushing my face away gently.

When the tears slip out of my eyes, I'm thankful he's already gone.

## 7
## KAI

*I* pushed her too hard. But if I don't push her, who will. She's certainly not about to pull herself out of the box she's crawled into to die. Every time I see her, it's as if she's given up a tiny bit more of herself to those bastards, letting them win even though they are gone. I hate it. The dead solemn look in her eyes eats at me, reminds me of feeling powerless, and that's something I don't allow myself.

When she ventures out of her room, the light outside is low and gray. The only light inside is the dappled firelight as it casts shadows across the walls. I watch her as she very pointedly avoids looking my way.

I'm stretched out in an oversized armchair with my feet propped on the solid wood coffee table and my laptop balanced on a pillow covering my thighs. I track her progress as she enters the kitchen, the long sleeves of her black sweater wrapped over her hands, so I only see her white fingertips poking out.

She grabs a bowl of fruit from the refrigerator and closes the door softly, making as little noise as possible, trying to make herself invisible.

That's impossible. I could never unsee her. Never forget she's there. If anything, her soft, clean scent is enough to keep her around, but she's so much more than that. More than she gives herself credit for.

"You can't ignore me forever," I say, not needing to raise my voice.

She stops in her progress back to her room and turns to face me but keeps her eyes down on the bowl clutched in her hands. The sweater is too big on her, hanging loose around her thighs. She's also wearing fluffy gray socks she's pulled up almost over her knees. "I'm not ignoring you. I just have nothing to say to you." Each word is crisp, clipped, and cheerless. Not that I expect her to be particularly cheerful. I never have.

I wave at the couch across from the fire. "Great, why don't you take a seat and talk to me then?"

Her eyes dart to me finally, then to the couch, and back to me. "Why?"

I shrug, snapping my laptop closed and tucking it between the chair cushion and the arm. "Why not? It's going to be just us here for a while. We should talk to each other."

She resettles her shoulders as if preparing for a physical fight. "You've been fine to leave me to my own devices up till now. Why do you want to get to know me all of a sudden? I'm not going to fuck you."

I scoff. "Oh, well, at least we've cleared that up. Little Rose, if I wanted to fuck you, there is very little you could do about it."

Her eyes lock on mine, her lip curling. "You'd do that, knowing how much I've been through."

I surge to my feet and make it around the couch before she even realizes I've moved. I grab her around the waist and haul her against me so I can stare down into her eyes. "No, I wouldn't do that to you. You misunderstand me." I lower my voice and dip in closer till my lips are only a breath away from hers. "If I wanted to fuck you, I'd have you so fucking wet you'd be climbing me like a tree, begging me to take you."

Her eyes are wide now, and I can see the heavy thump of her pulse in her throat. Is she aroused or scared? Probably both since I can't read it on her face. I release her slowly, so she doesn't slip off-balance. When my hands are off her skin, it's as if I can still feel her there, the soft, clean scent of her surrounding me, calming me in a way I don't understand, or maybe I'm not ready to.

I step backward once, then sit down in the chair again. "Anyway, as I was saying. Sit...please."

She swallows hard, her throat working, then skirts around the other end of the couch to sit as far away from me as possible. I scan her features, her body, trying to pick up on what she's feeling, but I can't tell, not with the darkness and the way she hides in oversized clothing without ever meeting my eyes. "What do you want to talk about?" Her voice is soft, still angry with me then.

I dig in the pocket of my sweatpants and pull out a burner phone. There's only one number programmed in it, and I hit it and press the phone to my ear.

Rose's brows draw down, matching a frown spread across her full lips. "Really, you tell me to sit, put on that whole show, and then you make a phone call—"

I hold up my hand when someone says hello on the other end of the line.

"Valentina, please."

Adrian doesn't say anything to me. There's a long pause, and then her soft voice answers. "Hello?"

"Valentina, it's Kai. I thought you and Rose might want to have a little chat."

Valentina gasps. "Yes, please."

I hit the speaker button and stand to grab the seat next to Rose. Just to piss her off, I throw myself on the couch right next to her, so close her bare thigh presses against mine.

"Go ahead," I prompt.

Rose stares at the phone, then at me. I see something more than fear there now, and I wonder if I've made a mistake. Maybe she's not ready. Maybe…

Rose clears her throat heavily. "Hello?"

Valentina makes some sort of noise on the line, forcing static. "Oh, my god, it's so good to hear your voice. You have no idea. I thought you were dead, or I would have been there for you the entire time. Please believe me."

Rose scans my face, which I keep neutral since we are not having that kind of argument right now. "No, it's okay. I understand. I wasn't ready to see anyone for a long time anyway."

"Are you okay? Is Kai being nice to you?"

I snort and roll my eyes even though she can't see me. Rose answers, staring at me while she does. "Oh yeah, he's the nicest, sweetest, most caring person, with the gentlest bedside manner you could ever meet."

Valentina laughs, making more static as if she can't press the phone to her face hard enough. "Yeah, that sure sounds like him. But what else, do you need anything, are you okay? I know things are weird right now, but soon, we'll be able to see each other, I promise. I miss you so much."

Rose swallows hard and stares at the phone as if she's afraid to look anywhere else, especially at me. "I miss you too, Val. I can't wait to see you."

"Then once all this blows over, maybe you and I can desecrate my father's and Sal's graves."

Rose freezes, her entire body tight like a bowstring. "W-What?"

"Sal and my father. They are both dead, and they deserve what they got. I know you didn't get the closure you probably needed, so we can do whatever you need to get that."

Rose drags her eyes to mine. The fire there is gone. Now they are haunted, empty—the look I hate more than anything. She snaps the phone out of my hand and throws it across the room, barely missing the fire by inches. When I look at her again, she's already gone, storming up to her room with her fruit still clutched tight in her grasp.

Val's voice comes from across the room. I heave myself off the couch and grab the phone off the soft throw rug in front of the fire. "Valentina?"

"Yes, I'm here. What happened? Where's Rose?"

I eye the landing in front of her door. "I think I fucked that up pretty badly. She didn't know they were dead. Should I have told her? I guess, but I wasn't sure how, or if you or Adrian would do it. Hell, she'd only begun speaking in full sentences to me in the first place."

"Oh, Kai, someone should have told her. But why is she angry? You'd think she'd be happy they're gone."

I stare at the door, one hand holding the phone, the other on my hip. "I think your cousin might be a little more bloodthirsty than you."

"What's that supposed to mean?"

I take my seat again, the laptop cold against my leg. "I think she was holding out to kill the bastards herself. I wonder if she planned to kill your father or just Sal."

Valentina sucks in a shocked breath. "What? No, Rose couldn't do something like that."

I keep my thoughts to myself because the Rose I've been getting to know could absolutely kill those men, and she'd delight in it. And I wouldn't blame her one bit.

"So what now?" she asks.

I shake my head and turn my attention to the blazing fire. "We wait things out, and maybe we can find some way to help her get through this."

"Besides this incident, is she okay? Anything else wrong?"

"Nothing you need to worry about. I have it under control, and I'll protect her with my life, you know that."

We sit in silence for a minute, only the crackle of the fire breaking it up. Then she whispers, "Keep her safe. That's all I ask. I hope we get you back home soon, Kai. Adrian misses you."

I smile because I can hear in her voice she misses me too, but she wouldn't dare say it with Adrian likely breathing down her neck. "I miss everyone too. I'll be home soon with Rose. Don't worry about me."

Adrian's deep voice answers this time. "We aren't worried, you bastard. We're pissed that these steps are even necessary. Get the shit cleaned up and get home."

I smile and hang up. It's good to hear they both miss me. That they both care. When I stand, I toss the phone into the fire and go up to find Rose.

The door isn't locked when I test the handle. I find her sitting against the balcony windows, staring out at the snow. It's finally stopped, but several feet have piled up outside, almost blocking the view from where she's sitting.

I sit on the edge of her rumpled bed. "What was that all about?"

She doesn't look at me, only continues drawing idle patterns on the fogged glass of the window. "I hate this. I hate that I'm the victim again. I hate that now they are gone, and I can't make them feel, even for one second, what they put me through." There's an edge to her tone, a bite, and I respect it. Hearing it almost makes me hard.

I cross the room to crouch next to her to see her face better. "But in the end, they are the ones who are dead, and you're still alive."

"Big whoop when I'm sitting here locked away on a mountain, afraid to talk to people or go outside." She turns to face me, dropping her hand onto her upturned knee. "I thought, maybe, by getting my revenge, it might bring me back to myself. It might help me become the person I used to be. Not this terrified…"

She trails off, and I sit down and pull her into my arms. She stiffens, her shoulders tight and rigid. "I told you not to touch me."

"Well, tough shit, because I plan to touch you. Often. Every day. Exposure therapy is a thing. Look it up. At the very least, we can take away some of that fear a little at a time."

She stays stiff as I hold her against me. "I don't think it's working."

"Patience."

After another minute, she tugs out of my hold. "Don't touch me."

This time, I reach out to grab her chin, and she slaps my hand away.

I smile. Her face shifts from anger to confusion. "What?"

I get to my feet and walk out. Let her think about it on her own for a while.

## 8

# ROSE

*I* can feel his hands on my skin, and I close my eyes against his face in the darkness. It's my only defense. I learned a long time ago that he only hurts me worse when I fight back. Or he throws in a little humiliation for the extra effort on his part. Something tangles around my feet, and I think he's tying me up. He's never done that before because I stopped fighting him, and I just let him do what he wants.

No. I can't let him tie me up. This time, I struggle, fighting the dry scratch of his hands as he shoves my thighs apart. Something else wraps around my arms, but I can't see it. All I can feel is the restriction and him. His hands are still prying my thighs apart so hard I'll have bruises where his fingers dig in.

"Stop!" I scream. Since I don't usually speak during these...attacks...I expect him to at least hesitate, but he doesn't. Nothing gets through, and I slap my arms up, shoving now, the former restriction stripped away from my wrists but still trapping my feet.

Tears flow down my cheeks now, and I'm mumbling, "Stop, stop, stop-stopstopstopstop," but nothing changes. Not the hard press on my thighs or my legs, not the acrid scent of his breath in my face or the rigid grip of his hands.

There's nothing I can do, and if I have to go through this again, I'm not going to survive a second time.

I scream, a loud shriek that rings in my ears, and then I open my eyes. The room is bright despite the darkness out the window. Somehow, the snow out my window brings in light on its own.

I'm in my bed. Alone. My face is wet, my cheeks, my neck. My hands are wrapped in my blanket, my feet trapped in the sheet I'd kicked toward the end of my bed.

I let out a ragged sob and shake my hands out of the bedding, then tug my feet loose, so I'm lying in the sweat-soaked bed with my T-shirt bunched around my waist. I stare down my body, my stomach still scarred and in some places pink from Sal's attack.

I'd been having a nightmare about being back there. Stuck again under his control with no way out.

The nightmares had been going away. At least, I thought they had. Maybe talking to Valentina today, hearing those bastard's names, brought things back up for me. I slow my breathing, focusing on taking long deep breaths even as my heart pounds in my chest.

When I heard they were dead, all I could think about was I'd never get to kill them myself. I'd never make them feel the pain they'd made me feel. But now, staring at the white ceiling, I wonder whether Kai made the right choice in keeping it from me. For not telling Valentina the truth about my survival?

No. Obviously, I'm not as far along in my recovery as I thought. Would dealing with them myself have given me the closure I needed to actually put the past behind me?

I curl on my side and roll up to sit. Everything in my body aches, even my scalp. From the screaming or the tangle in the sheets, I don't know.

When I get my heart rate under control, I stand, head to the balcony doors, and throw them open wide. Puffs of snow from the piles against the door fall onto the floor, peppering my bare feet. It doesn't matter. I can't feel anything but the deeply rooted body ache that radiates from my bones.

The soft, freezing wind against my legs doesn't even do anything to jump-start me from the stupor. I'm so tired of this numbness, of alternating between nothing and intense pain with no middle ground. So fucking tired.

I sit on the end of the bed and cradle my head in my hands. The second I close my eyes, the nightmare surges up and, along with it, a wave of nausea.

No.

I lift my face again so the cold air can cut through it all, at least enough so I won't throw up on my bedroom floor.

The air starts to help, but a deep rage takes the place of the nausea in my gut. They took my revenge from me, and no one said a word about it, thinking I didn't get a say in how their ugly little lives ended.

Did Valentina know, or did her new husband and Kai decide to take care of things on their own? It's a question I want an answer to, along with the details on how they died. I want to know every little detail, but mostly, I want to know how much they suffered. It would never be enough, but I still need to hear it.

Standing is hard, between the ache in my bones and the heavy grating anger firing through me. I'm a little dizzy and stumble on the way to the bedroom door, tripping over my ripped-off blankets. My shoulder hits the door first, and I lean into it as I cup the door handle.

My knees are shaking, and I stare down at my fingers also shaking as I attempt to open the door. I don't get anywhere, and I realize it's because I'm leaning on it. It takes a minute to get my feet under me, and I try again. Nothing. The door doesn't budge.

I'm trapped.

This is another nightmare, right? I shake the knob, but nothing happens.

No. I can't be trapped. No. No.

I jerk the door, slamming my hand into it as if that will shimmy it loose from the frame despite my desperate tug on the cold brass knob.

"Open, fucking open!" I yell, knowing if anyone else were here, I'd sound like a fucking psychopath right now. Between the screaming and the yelling at inanimate objects, I'm prime for the nuthouse.

It doesn't matter because I know Kai won't let me go. Adrian, Valentina, no one will let me go anywhere, even if I wanted to.

I am just as trapped by my own mind as I am by the people around me, the people who claim they are protecting me. We left the city because of the danger, and now I'm even more trapped on a mountain in the snow with nowhere to go and no way out except by Kai's grace and help.

How did I allow this? "Open up! Please fucking open up!" I shout at the door, pounding on it, then slamming the flat of my fist against it even though it stings.

I don't care if it hurts. One more pain in the wash of it through my body at the moment. One more sensation that will dull later, leaving me empty and hopeless.

A sob rips from my throat, and I clasp my red hand over my mouth, stifling another one. No, I might scream, but I won't let them see me cry, not today, not so fresh after that nightmare.

A laugh bubbles up from some unhinged part of me, merging with my tears. There's no one here to see me cry. No one to care if I'm raving like a crazy person or throwing myself off the cold, snowy balcony to be bear food. No one gives a shit, and maybe they'd be better off without me.

I cast my eyes back toward the balcony doors, curling my hand around my jaw now, needing to hold on to something.

Pounding reaches me from somewhere, echoing through the room and in my own head. It takes me a minute to realize I'm not hitting the door anymore, then another second for the door to shake enough that I take a few steps back.

It slams inward, hitting the wall hard, and I'm grabbed up in two heavy hands before I can get my bearings. I fight on instinct now, never again letting myself be the complacent little victim Sal turned me into before the end.

I slam my hand up into a face, a man's face by the stubble on his jaw, and scramble back, but he's got me off-balance, or maybe that's me between the pain and the nightmares, off-balance and unhinged.

I hit the ground hard, only saved from a solid head knock by the covers I'd left on the floor when I scrambled for the door earlier.

The hands grab my arms, and I fight, squeezing my eyes closed, scratching, clawing, whatever it takes to get the weight of the man off my body and away from me.

Deep cursing comes from him, but I don't give an inch, using my legs and heels to dig into his calves, his feet, kicking, anything to make him release me so I can get away.

A muffled, "Fuck," is uttered almost against my face, which makes me struggle harder.

"For fuck's sake, Rose, wake the hell up," Kai says in my face, his hot breath fanning against my mouth.

I open my eyes and scan his face, taking in his features, needing to see it's him and no one else. It doesn't matter. I'd have still fought even him, but now I freeze, going still under him, loosening the hold I have on his legs with mine.

He leans in so he can stare into my eyes. His eyes look almost black in the dark. "What the fuck are you doing?"

I try to force an answer, to explain, anything, but no words come out. Another hot shameful tear rolls down my cheek. His eyes shift to track it, then his hands loosen on their hold around my wrists.

"Fuck," he whispers, this time with less vehemence.

I shudder underneath him, for the first time feeling exactly how our bodies fit together, how his heavy muscled weight is aligned with my body exactly where he'd be if he intended to…

I rotate my wrists, intent on peeling them out of his grasp, which only makes him tighten his hold. "Hold on a moment."

Leaning up to get in his face, I yell, "Get the fuck off me now."

Of course, he doesn't move, and I didn't expect him to either. His eyes narrow, and he only settles against me harder as if he'd been holding back some of his weight before. "You don't give me orders, Rose. I'll get off you when I damn well please, especially after you wake me the hell up with whatever the hell kind of episode you were having in here.

They haven't been that bad since the first few nights after your recovery. What's going on?"

I just glare at him. Since he won't get off me, I don't intend to tell him a single thing until he does at least that much.

His voice takes a lower note. Almost a whisper, but it washes through me. "I can stay right here between your pretty thighs all night. Don't tempt me."

That tone starts something deep in my belly, arousal. I don't have much experience with it, especially where another person is concerned. The acrid bile in my throat and the heat at my core melding together sends me into a tailspin.

I buck my hips up, trying to get him off me again, but all that accomplishes is settling him more firmly between my legs, allowing me to feel every solid inch of his body and his dick against my core.

"Careful," he breathes, like a threat and a warning all at once.

# 9

## KAI

*I* pitch my voice low in an attempt at calming when she thrashes underneath me like a wild animal. "Stop fucking struggling, or I'll give you a reason to fear me."

For a second, she freezes, unmoving, her eyes, pupils blown and boring into mine. I tighten my hold on her wrists, only enough to keep myself in check. Every inch of her body lies along mine, and I find myself wanting to savor another person for the first times in a long time. Even before everything happened with the council bitch, I didn't really want anyone to touch me.

I guess touching her is not the same as her touching me. But the fucking scent of her. Soft, clean soap with a hint of sweat, no doubt from the nightmare I heard earlier. "Are you done fighting?"

She drops her gaze to my mouth, scanning my face, and I'm not sure what she's seeing or what she's looking for. Either way, I can't take much longer lying in the cradle of her thighs like this, at least not without causing her to panic all over again.

Her voice is soft and scratchy when she finally answers me. "I couldn't get out of the room."

I don't bother to hide my annoyance. "Yeah, because you were being pissy at me and locked the door. You must have woken after your nightmare and completely forgotten. You can't keep going on like this, Rose. It's not healthy, not for you, and certainly not for me."

Her brows bunch together, and she shakes her head. "What's that supposed to mean? Like I have any control over this. You think I want to wake up in cold sweats with my scars aching? You think I want to have nightmares that make me scream so loud my throat hurts when I wake up?"

I lean in so I can meet her eyes head-on. "No, so don't deliberately misunderstand what I'm saying. You can take control over so many things in your life, things you're refusing to acknowledge."

"Like what?" she spits. "I can't go anywhere on my own. I can't stand when people touch me. Even now, my skin is crawling from you up against me."

Ouch. I should be offended because of the slight note of disgust in her tone, but I've learned enough about her that she's only saying it to drive me away. Yes, she might have been touched, but she doesn't hate me, even if she wishes she did.

"You can curse me and call me anything you like. It won't stop me from protecting you or from helping you."

Her response is sullen, a pout on her full pink lips. "I don't need your help."

I tipped my chin toward the broken doorframe. "Yeah, you can't even get out of your bedroom, but you don't need my help."

It was the wrong thing to say, like poking an already shaking beehive. This time, she doesn't yell. She barely whispers, her eyes full of fire and fury. "Fuck you, and fuck Adrian. Fuck all of you. I don't need any of you."

I press her hands down into the floor harder. "What about Valentina?" God, I can't believe I'm about to say this to her face, but it's a truth she's long since needed to hear. "What about the woman who considers you a sister? Family? The only reason she came back that night, the only reason Sal got his fucking hands on her, was because she'd never leave you. Adrian asked her to stay with him, asked why, if she accepted his help, would she go back home. Tell me, Rose? Why would she go back to that house?"

I feel like the fucking monster so many say I am. Shame curls in my gut like a sleeping dragon waiting patiently for a weak moment to strike.

Her eyes are wide again, her breathing a little too fast. "Wha—What are you saying? That it's my fault she almost died? That I nearly got her killed."

I grind my teeth together. It wasn't her fucking fault. It was Sal's for being a psychopath with a small dick, but I can't tell her that. I need her to start seeing how her actions and reactions affect those around her. Adrian would kill her without a second thought if she did something to hurt Valentina in one of her rages. And then Valentina would never forgive him. Her loss would break him, and I'd never allow that.

So right now, I'll play the monster so he won't have to.

I clear my features and shake my head, curling my lip so she sees disgust even though it's only shame and anger constricting my chest. "She could have left with him and never once had to deal with Sal or her father again. She only came back for you."

She blinks once, twice, and a fat tear slides down her cheek, then another. "No, I mean…" Her eyes turn pleading, begging me to take it back or make it all better, but I can't, not this time. Not when she needs to understand she can't keep going on like this. Especially when I can finally reunite her with her cousin.

"Why would you say something so horrible?"

It takes work—years of facing society and playing a part—to keep my face neutral. "You need to hear it. All of it. You wanted the truth, and it's time you start hearing it."

I go silent, watching the emotions roll across her features one after the other like a computer code autoloading in front of my eyes.

I wait for her to call me names or say something to defend herself, but when she doesn't, I loosen my hold on her hands, intent on letting her up and freeing her so we can get her room cleaned up, and at least one of us can get back to sleep.

Her slap comes out of nowhere and cracks across my cheek so hard I see stars. I grab her wrists and pin her again sheerly out of reflex, my muscles going tight as if waiting for another blow. When her head lifts off the ground, I simply react again, one hand scooping her wrists together while the other circles her throat to keep her pinned and prevent her from smashing her face into mine if she were so inclined. And the wild rage in her eyes right now says she might just do it if she knew she could inflict some pain.

"What the fuck was that for?"

She grinds her teeth together, pressing into my hand, trying to break free of my hold. But she's been recovering too long, not using her body, growing weak. She can barely move her head side to side, let alone off the hardwood.

"Stop fighting me, and I'll let you up. This is the kind of behavior I'm referring to. You don't have to just fucking hit people when you're pissed. I get you're all rage and anger at the moment, and I understand it more than you know, but it won't solve anything. Use your fucking brain for a minute and not your heart."

She scoffs. "You say that like you have a heart. You're the one who has been all over me since we got here. You keep touching me, pushing me, so this fight-or-flight mode, as my doctor calls it, is your fault."

I blink and lean in, a slow grin curling the side of my cheek. "My fault, huh? Was it my fault back in the apartment too, when I never saw you but got reports from others about broken furniture, dishes, anything you could destroy to calm your anger?"

A red wash tinges her cheeks. There. At least she's fucking ashamed and knows, even if she doesn't want to admit she's out of control.

I keep pushing, though, because it's what she needs. "Did you know Valentina is pregnant? It occurs to me that no one would have told you except me."

Her legs which had been trying to scramble upward to buck me off her go still, and she almost stops breathing. "Pregnant? How?"

I level her a look. "You really want me to explain the birds and the bees to you? Pretty sure you can figure out the mechanics."

She swallows hard, and I feel it under my palm. When it seems like she's not going to head butt me, I pull my hand off her neck and brace it above her shoulder to pull some of my weight off her chest. "Now, we are going to do this slowly. I'm going to get up, and you're not going to come at me like some crazed wildcat. Got it?"

Her nod isn't very comforting, but it's a risk I'll have to take, even if it's my balls that will likely take the brunt of her anger first.

I lean into her chest again so I can release her hands, but she's already trying to scramble out from underneath me, rubbing the soft skin of her thighs along mine. I can smell her cunt with her legs wide open, and my mouth waters for a taste.

But I can't touch her, not now. Not while she's terrified of everyone who lays a finger on her. It's as if she expects every touch to turn into a lie, each one to become darker, dangerous, hurtful.

"Wildcat, what did I say about slow?"

She huffs, her breath fanning across my face. "Well, get the hell off me, and then I'll get off the floor as slow as you like."

I tighten my hold on her wrists again, my hips shifting ever so slightly against hers as I try to rebalance my weight. The heat of her, fucking hell, I can't handle this. I don't want sex. After what I endured, hell, I don't even want to be around a fucking woman. But Rose doesn't feel the same to me. Even after everything, she feels safe. She feels like home. Sometimes even more so when she's spitting and raging.

"Stop fucking struggling, or you are not going to like what happens."

She tips her chin up, staring down her nose at me, even while flat on her back. Despite her trials and suffering, she's still a princess to the core. "What's that supposed to mean?"

I arch into her on purpose this time and revel in the way she sucks in a heavy breath. "Because I'm hard as a fucking rock, and if you keep testing my control, you'll learn it's not infinite."

I stare into her wide eyes, and for a second, I imagine the jump in her pulse isn't just fear, that maybe, somewhere in there, she can feel me against her and want me too.

But then, as I feared earlier, her face comes up, and she smacks me right in the goddamn nose with her forehead. I release her and roll off her body to lie on my back, holding the bridge of my nose to stifle the flare of pain shooting into my eye sockets.

Fucking wildcat indeed.

I blink my eyes open to roll over and look at her, but she's already standing, and she heads to the door. She darts one scared look my way, then bolts out the door as if she can outrun me.

As if she can fight me.

As if she can hide from me.

I check that my nose isn't bleeding and hop to my feet easily enough. At least it's not broken. I didn't relish hunting down the medical supplies for the cabin in the middle of the night.

Stepping into the hall, I breathe softly, slowly, while listening carefully. I hear a rustle toward the kitchen and smile to myself. "Little wildcat, why don't you come out and talk to me? If I have to hunt you down, you will not like the consequences."

Of course, she says nothing.

I adjust my hard-on in my boxer briefs and start down the stairs.

She has no idea what she's unleashed.

# 10

## ROSE

*I* shouldn't have run. I tuck my knees into my chest and drag the collar of my T-shirt up over my nose to stifle my heavy breathing. Even through the thin material, it sounds so loud. Too loud. He'll find me any second.

I shouldn't have run. There's nowhere to go, nowhere he won't find me.

Hell, while I'm reconsidering the last few minutes, I shouldn't have fought him. Yet as I huddle against a pantry shelf, a bag of flour digging into my back, I can't bring myself to regret it.

I never fight. It had always been easier to just give in and let Sal do what he wanted with me so I could get away sooner. Even on that last night, I didn't fight.

I almost bled out, knowing I didn't do a damn thing to prevent it. That bastard almost killed me, and I almost let him.

Stifling a quiet sob with my hands doubled over my mouth, on the outside of my T-shirt, I watch the pantry door handle waiting for it to rattle.

Any second now.

He might find me, but I won't make it easy for him. Not this time.

I close my eyes, and I can still feel Kai on top of me. The memory of it doesn't give me the same panic haze as the actual act did.

Calmer now, I feel a hot wash of shame crawl up my neck. He hadn't hurt me. He was trying to keep me from hurting myself.

I smother another wash of shame, combined with a slow roll of nausea.

He hadn't hurt me, but I'd hurt him, lashing out at anything, everything.

Hell, if I were him, I'd toss my ungrateful ass out into the snow.

Relaxing my hands, I let them fall away from my face, my T-shirt slipping back down under my chin. There's a moment of silence, nothing like the sounds of the city where there's always noise coming from somewhere.

Maybe I'm an idiot. Another long moment passes, and I start to feel foolish, silly for sitting in my underwear in the dark pantry, freezing my ass off on the floor.

Then I catch the soft shuffle of bare feet on the hardwood and tense. What will he do to me when he finds me, and I have no doubt he will?

I snatch the tall peppermill from the nearest shelf, eyeing the large cans of tomatoes as well, and clutch it to my chest.

We haven't learned a lot about each other. Well, he knows everything about me, and I know hardly anything about him. But something in the back of my mind, a primal voice, tells me that when he catches me, he'll make me pay for running.

The truly scary part is, there's a tiny—oh so tiny—part of me waiting for the moment, wondering what he'll do, and not in an I have to claw my way to safety kind of way.

The shuffle comes closer.

I swallow hard and hug the peppermill to my chest. It won't do much but having some kind of weapon feels better than having nothing.

A slight shadow breaks up the very faint light coming from under the door. Shit. I don't know if I should close my eyes or run or scream. All of it. None of it.

The handle turns once, and the door jerks open, revealing Kai, still in nothing but his boxer briefs, towering over me, wearing a stern look of disapproval on his face.

I don't give him time to react before I throw the peppermill at him and scramble around his legs to try to get out of the doorway.

The mill crashes to the floor beside me, and I barely have a second of freedom before a hard, hot hand clamps around my ankle.

"Where do you think you're going?"

Instinctively, I kick out, trying to dislodge his hold, maybe buy myself a few more seconds, but his grip is iron around my bones. He presses his hand tighter, showing me how much further he could push it.

"Rose, stop this. You're being ridiculous,"

I don't know if it's the condescension in his tone or the grip he's loosened just enough. Instead of answering, I kick out hard enough to send him flat on his ass. This time, I move faster, crawl faster, intent on getting back to my bedroom.

I don't even get to my feet before his hands clamp around one of my ankles and lower calf.

I struggle, but this time, he's not giving an inch, and if I keep trying, he's going to break something. He shifts his grip just enough to keep me on my knees, sliding across the smooth wood until I fall over onto my ass. Not that it's stopped him. He continues to drag me across the floor until the carpet in front of the fireplace is bunched up under my ass, my panties following suit.

All I can do is stare up at him, ringed by the light of the very faint embers still nestled in the hearth. "What do you want from me?"

I'm proud that my voice doesn't shake, and that I don't scream at him again.

He shifts my ankle to one hand and throws a couple of logs in the fireplace with the other hand. They hit the embers, sparking a small flame that grows larger by the second.

I give my leg a gentle tug, which earns me a glare over his shoulder. I blink and stare at those impossibly wide shoulders, corded with muscles. I mean, this isn't the first time I've seen him with some clothes off, but I've never really studied him before, not like this.

The fear from earlier is bleeding away. If he wants to keep hold of me as punishment, then it's not the worst thing I've had to endure. I settle onto the soft carpet, shifting it so I can lay flat at least.

When the fire blazes high, he turns to face me.

Something in his eyes kindles the panic, the fear, in my chest again. I make a move to try to get free again, but his eyes warn me against it.

"Don't you fucking dare move." His tone is fire, fury, ferocity that I have no touchstone for.

Yes, I'd been brutalized repeatedly, but there had never been any anger in it. Most of the time, I suspected Sal only hurt me because he couldn't hurt my cousin. A power play more than vengeance.

I swallow hard and stare at him, the light is brighter now, and I can see his chest, his abs, all that muscle leading down to—

Shit. He's pissed and so fucking hard I can almost see the tip of his dick busting out of the top of his boxer briefs.

"Um." It's all I get out before he's on top of me. Not the gentle, yielding way he'd been before when he'd tried to keep me from hurting myself and him. No, there is no give in his body now. Nothing but hard lines demanding I do the yielding this time.

My mouth is dry, my throat a barren desert. I can only blink at him.

He makes a subtle shift, and then I feel it. The thick, so very hard length of him right there, nothing but our underwear separating our bodies from each other.

My breathing sounds louder between us, borderline panting as panic threatens to take hold and carry me off again.

I shove at his chest, but it's no use. He won't move. His eyes tell me what my body already knows. Yet I can't keep from fighting. I won't let another man kill me without a fight.

I wrap my legs around his hips and try to set him off-balance, but that doesn't work either. My breathing is coming faster now in short, fast bursts of air that feel like they are doing nothing for me.

"Why are you doing this? Please get off me." I hate the whine in my tone and the panic in my voice.

He leans in until our faces are almost touching. "Stop fucking moving. We aren't doing this song and dance again."

There's a red mark on his cheek and a smear of blood beneath. Did I do that? I stare, wide-eyed, still freaking the fuck out, but reality slowly snakes in to break through.

Who the hell am I that I'd hurt him when he'd done nothing to me except try to help me? How am I this person now?

I swallow against my parched throat. "Look, I'm sorry about—"

"No, that's not what this is about. I don't want your apologies or your excuses. You need to fucking do better, and until I see that, none of the rest of it matters."

Shit. More of the panic recedes, enough that I can extend my inhales, lengthen my exhales, and get some control over myself.

A hot tear rolls down my cheek, but I don't swipe it away, keeping my eyes on his. "What if it doesn't work? What if this is me now?"

For a second, the world stops as I wait for his answer. But nothing comes. He shifts his head to the side and buries his face into the crook of my neck.

I freeze, my heart beating harder, but for an entirely different reason. "Wh-What are you doing?"

He sucks in a loud breath, and his chest presses me harder into the rug. Is he...smelling me?

I shift, which only reminds me exactly where we are, and exactly how our bodies fit together, and exactly how much I don't actually hate this.

Not as much as I should anyway.

"Stop moving," he says into the curve of my neck. His nose brushes my ear, sending a little tingle through me. "If you don't stop wiggling around like that, I'm going to strip that scrap of fabric off your cunt and fuck you until I've had my fill of you."

A hot awareness rolls through me, igniting long-dormant corners of my body. At the same time, nausea follows, threatening to send me free-falling back into panic mode. "You wouldn't do that to me. You wouldn't take that from me, not after everything I've been through."

He lifts his face to look at me again. His eyes seem darker now. "What, in our very short acquaintance, has made you believe I'm a good man?"

I swallow so loudly I can hear it, even over the crackle of the fire.

He shifts his hips, hiking his body into mine. The hard straight length of him brushes along my panties from my asshole to my clit.

It's like a damn jumper cable to every nerve, every muscle, every cell inside me. They are awake…and worse—they want.

I want.

Which is something I'm not prepared for. Not in the least, since every time something sexual comes to mind, all I can think about is Sal.

He moves again, pressing into me harder. I wait for the pain, but all I feel is pleasure as his clothed head brushes right over my clit and back again.

"Fuck," he whispers, his head falling down to the curve of my neck again. "You feel so good. I can't even imagine what you'd feel like clenched around me right now."

I make a noise, and it takes me a minute to realize I'd whimpered. Actually whimpered at the idea of him inside me.

This time, he shifts his hips, keeping the motion of dragging himself along my body, back and forth.

I reach out and hold his shoulders, warring between shoving him away and pulling him in tighter.

My first thought is if I lay here, he'll finish, and then it will be over. But there's something about him on top of me, every inch of him igniting every inch of me, that keeps me awake. Keeps me from dissociating and putting the distance I've always needed between us.

He moves one more time, and I cry out, more a sigh than a whimper this time, at least.

This breaks the spell. He shoves up on his hands, so he's over me but not touching, except where my legs are still wrapped around his hips. "Go to bed, Rose, before I do something we'll both regret."

## 11

## KAI

*E*very new look at her, every new touch of her skin, every taste of her I get is another pebble in the pond, slowly weighing me down. I need to stop this now before it's too late, and I ruin us both. She's still asleep as I quietly pass her closed door and head down to the fitness room.

I've thrown myself into working out as I usually do when I'm stressed, but it's not working this time. I unwrap a cherry Tootsie Pop, put in my earbuds, and focus on the burn in my muscles.

It's been three days since I last touched her. To her credit, she's taking it better than the last time, and I'm not pushing her on things like I usually do. Hell, she probably appreciates the break.

After doing so many push-ups that my arms give out and leave my belly flopping on the mat, I relax, letting myself sink into the rubber and bring my breathing back to normal. I close my eyes, and the scent of her hits me first. So hard I have to open them again and look up to make sure she's not standing in the doorway.

Of course she's not. She'd never seek me out first. Well, maybe if she wanted to scream at me.

Rolling over, I run my hands down the ridge of my erection. I'd been sporting the same one since I ignored it when I woke up. I can't cross that line with her because there's no going back. Not for either of us.

I slowly roll my hand up and down my shaft, still tucked safely in my shorts. If she weren't so broken, if she hadn't been through so much, I might have considered offering her an arrangement. Mutual pleasure between friends.

It sounds good in my head, but in reality, I know if I touch her, I won't ever stop. Especially when I feel how her tight little body grips me. How she'll say my name when she comes. I've imagined that more times than I care to admit over the past couple of days.

How do I scrub her out of my mind when she seems to be branded there? Her scent, the quiet way she walks, all of it. It's utterly ridiculous, considering how little we know about each other. And how much Adrian and Valentina will rip my head off if I hurt Rose.

I sit up, leaving my aching cock to roll on my belly again to start another round of push-ups. I can only do a few before my muscles give out completely. I wipe the sweat from my brow and lumber to my feet, my thighs still screaming from yesterday's workout.

The second she walks past the door, I can smell her, like clean sheets and sun-warmed lavender. I pull my earbuds out and listen as she makes herself a bowl of cereal.

We only have a few more days until I'll have to send an associate out for supplies and meet them to restock. At least some of the perishables.

I try to picture her in the kitchen but then decide to walk out and just see what she's up to. We'd been avoiding each other in one way or another since we got here. It's not her fault I want to bend her over the counter and make her scream my name.

She's sitting on that very counter I've fantasized about, swinging her legs but never letting her feet hit the lower cabinets. I smile and trek my gaze up the long line of her bared legs. "Having fun?"

She jumps and sloshes cereal milk onto her hand. "What the hell? Don't sneak up on me like that."

I tuck my earbuds in my pocket and lean against the refrigerator. "I've been standing here for five minutes. You should be more perceptive."

With a scowl, she wipes her hand on a towel and resumes her position on the counter. "Excuse me, but I'm trying to enjoy my breakfast."

I let my gaze linger from her ankles to the sides of her bare thighs in her sleep shorts to the bra-less swell of her breasts. "Don't let me stop you."

This time, her look isn't as fierce, and I spot the hint of fear in her eyes.

That's my cue to head back to the weights. I'm about to tuck my earbuds in my ear when someone pounds on the heavy wood front door of the cabin.

I glance at Rose, who is frozen, her eyes wide. "Who is it?"

"How the hell should I know. I can't see them through the damn door." This earns me a glare, which I give right back.

The pounding comes again, and I reach up on top of the fridge and feel around for the holster I stashed there on our first day in the cabin.

"What's that?" Rose whispers.

I pull out the 9mm and keep it aimed at the floor. "What does it look like?"

She hops off the counter and meets me near the entryway to the kitchen. "Can I have a gun?"

I pin her with another glare. "What? No, of course not. It's my job to keep you safe."

She slides the cereal bowl onto the counter and crosses her arms under her breasts. "What if I want to keep myself safe? What if you get shot and killed, and then it's just me against an armed intruder?"

I nudge her farther into the kitchen with my hip. "Wait over there. Also, I've noted how much confidence you have in my abilities. I'll remember that for later."

Her breath hits my ear, and I sigh because she's not going to listen to a damn thing I say. "What's that supposed to mean? Later?"

The pounding starts again, this time more insistent. I creep toward the door, keeping both it and Rose in my sight. "Later," I whisper. "Means when I get my hand on your ass and spank you for that mouth."

She clamps her lips together, going rigid. Finally, I get her to shut up.

I check the lock on the door, spin the deadbolts, and then open the door with one hand, the weapon at the ready with the other.

The person on the other side, knee-deep in snow, is not someone I expected to see anytime soon. "Selena?"

My younger sister, Selena, raises one perfectly groomed eyebrow my way. "Are you going to let me in? I'm freezing my tits off out here!"

I start to open the door out of habit but then pause before revealing Rose. "What do you want?"

She waves at the house. "To go inside before I get frostbite on my nipples, how about that?"

I scowl. "So ladylike, much sophisticated."

That earns me an eye roll. "Well, big brother, I'm here to see you, so let me the fuck inside."

Rose is holding my bicep now, behind the door, staring off into space as she listens. I risk a glance her way, and she mouths, "Your sister?"

With another sigh, I make sure to keep my body there so she can't get around the frame and invite the menace of my family inside herself. "You should leave, Selena. This is supposed to be a safe house. No one is supposed to know where it is."

She grins. "Kind of difficult when I'm the one who brokered the sale on your behalf. Or did you forget you owe me big time?"

To be fair, I had forgotten she was the one who purchased the cabin, but I didn't think she'd ever show up here. I haven't seen Selena in years, not since she took over the council in Chicago. It allowed my parents to retire on a tropical island, and for me and my other sister, Julia, to hide in the shadows while Selena took center stage.

Neither of us minded one bit. We're both made for the shadows.

"What are you really doing here, Selena?" My patience is wearing thin, so asking her directly is the only way to get a straight answer out of her these days. Every time I talk to her, it's political climate this and what's best for our people that. "Don't you have a coup to organize or something?"

She shivers, wrapping her arms around herself, drawing the heavy gray fur coat tighter. "If you won't let me in, then I'm going to force you."

I don't have time to think about the words before she's shoving past me into the living room of the cabin. I spin, and she eyes the gun still clutched in my hand. "Really. Are you going to shoot me, Kai?" She cocks her head to study the weapon. "With a nine mill no less? I at least deserve a forty-five for having to stand in the snow for ten damn minutes."

Her gaze shifts to Rose, who is partially hiding behind me, partially peeking around my arms. "And who might you be?"

I don't answer, and when Rose opens her mouth, I step between the women. "You need to leave. You know you shouldn't be here in the first place."

She sweeps her fur coat open and out so she can sit down, her back against the couch, her legs crossed, one over the other. At least she's wearing boots, even if they are thousands of dollars and couture. "I'm not leaving until we've had a chance to chat and catch up."

I glare first, then shake my head. "I'm great. Things are good. It's time for you to leave now."

"Not going to cut it, Kai, and you know it." She sits forward and shucks the coat, then stands and skirts the couch to get a look at Rose. "Did you kidnap this sweet, little thing?"

Rose stiffens and then glares at my sister. Maybe she has more sense than I give her credit for.

Selena holds her hand out, which Rose reluctantly shakes. "I'm Selena Aquila, Kai's sister."

"Little sister," I amend.

She rolls her eyes, still staring at Rose. "Well, if maturity level is anything to go by, then I'm the older one."

Rose stares between us as we bicker.

I grab her coat and shove it toward her. "Time to go."

When she doesn't move to the door, I walk to it and throw the coat out into the falling snow. "How about now? Need to go rescue that, I'm sure it shouldn't get wet. Not with this blizzard coming."

She crosses her arms until I have to close the door again to keep Rose from shivering in her pajamas beside me.

"I told you, I'm not leaving yet. We need to talk, catch up."

I put the gun on the mantel and cross the room again to face her properly. Lord knows Mom would kill me if I shot my sister, even if she deserves it. "Why are you here? What do you really want?"

She studies me for a moment and then Rose in her pajamas. "I didn't get her name."

"That's because she didn't give it to you. Answer my question."

A small smile plays at the corner of Rose's mouth. Enough to make me shoot her a glare too. "Don't smile. This isn't funny. She could have been followed. Hell, she could have been paid to murder you, and I wouldn't be able to do a damn thing about it."

Her smile grows wider, and I huff and walk toward the fireplace to get away from them both.

Selena joins me a second later, the soft honeysuckle scent of her perfume almost gagging me. It's not a bad scent, but strong. All perfume seems that way to me these days. Too much for my senses, frying my sinuses. "I really did come to check on you, Kai. Let's chat a minute, and then I'll get out of your hair."

She sweeps her long brown curls over one shoulder and gives me her businesswoman smile.

"No, tell me one reason you are here first."

Her smile never wavers. "I'm here to talk you into turning yourself over to the council."

# 12
## ROSE

*I*'m not sure why, but I can't picture Kai with a sister. Not that they don't look anything alike, they have the same posture, the same confident *I don't give a fuck what you think about me* air.

Watching them both is like watching the world's sexiest ping pong match. They are both stunning, and it's hard to look away.

Selena resumes her seat on the couch, getting comfortable amidst the cushions. Acting for all the world like she didn't just drop a bomb in the middle of our living room. "What do you say, big brother, want to make my life easier?"

He gives her a little grin, one I recognize as a trap. "And why would I do that? I'm not under your jurisdiction. You have no say in what I do."

Selena leans forward and flashes her brother a pout. "That damn councilwoman in your city won't leave well enough alone. She calls almost every day asking if someone has apprehended you yet."

I shift my focus to Kai and watch as he smooths his features to cocky arrogance. "Well, what can I say? I'm memorable. She got one taste of me and kept coming back for more."

I can't pinpoint it, but there's something in Kai's voice as he said that, his attention solely on his sister now. "And I doubt she hates the idea of you being beholden to her or vice versa if you hand me over."

Selena puts on her best imitation of affronted, and it's actually so bad it's almost comical. This is so much better than soap operas. "You think I'd turn you over to her? Leave you hanging like that?"

Kai throws his long body in the chair and pins his sister with a glare. "Please, you're here, in my house, asking me to turn myself in, instead. If you thought for one minute that Mom wouldn't be at your door in a heartbeat if you turned me over, I'd already be in cuffs, stuffed into a helicopter."

I can't remember if Kai told me he'd been arrested by the council, was that where he'd been during that time he never showed up at the apartment? I turn back to the kitchen and hop up on the counter again to watch. They both seem oblivious to my presence as they verbally spar, and I don't mind one bit.

After a long, tense silence, Selena settles back into the couch again. "Actually, I am here to check on you, but mostly to make sure you're still alive. I'd get more inheritance after all, if you met a tragic end."

Kai makes a noise, like a grunt, but he's smiling, so there must be something I'm missing here. Valentina and I would do anything for each other, discussing a betrayal so openly doesn't make sense to me. At least not in this context.

I watch Kai as he studies his sister, scanning her face, her body, but in an assessing way, not tense, like the way he stares at me.

I sit forward, wrapping my arms around my knees to rest my chin on top. Shit. He does stare at me in a totally different way. Now that I think about it, he looks at me like I stare at a brand new box of frosted flakes.

A lump builds in my throat, and I swallow it, intent on watching them unnoticed while I can.

Selena stares into the fire. "I don't think they'd kill you, ya know? She didn't seem keen on execution. She might just lock you up for a bit. I'd put a good word in for you too, and I'm sure that would help."

The softness in Kai's eyes is gone now. "Not going to happen. Not in a million years. I'd rather be dead than under that woman's control again."

This seems to confuse Selena, and me too. What's so wrong with being locked up for a bit, at least until they prove Kai's innocence or find him a better place to hide. I glance around the cabin and wonder why he brought me here. He should have tons of houses across the country if his wardrobe is anything to go by.

Selena flips her hair over her shoulder and shifts into the couch deeper. "Anything I can do to convince you?"

Kai watches her get more and more comfortable, his frown deepening with every twitch. "No. Now you said what you came to say, it's time for you to leave."

I slide off the couch, wanting to step closer to Kai, not understanding why I have the sudden urge to touch him. People touching me was a no-go, but maybe, maybe touching him wouldn't be so bad.

I make it only a step before Selena continues with her goals. "I hear she has a state-of-the-art dungeon and free drugs to make her prisoners more comfortable."

When Kai grinds his jaw together, I can't resist anymore. I step up beside the chair and perch on the arm. "He said he's not going anywhere, and you're not going to be able to convince him."

Her deep brown eyes shift to me, the firelight caressing her soft dark skin. The same dark tan shade as Kai's. "What did you say to me? I don't even know who you are, and you're going to speak to me like that."

A part of me wants to cower, the part of me that's been hiding for months waiting to get better, waiting to be a little less broken, a little more me. But I'm starting to think it doesn't work that way. "He said no. You should leave it alone if you want to stay, or better yet, maybe you should go."

She narrows her eyes and slides to the edge of the couch like she might get up and do something, except she doesn't. I keep my eyes on her, and Kai is tense beside me in the chair. "Don't presume to know anything about me or my business. Even more so, don't presume you know anything about my brother I don't already know."

Kai cuts in before I can respond. "It doesn't matter what that woman says. I'm basically on parole. Adrian and Valentina vouched for me, and as far as she is concerned until the hearing comes back around, I'm a free man."

Selena tuts, actually tuts, at her brother and rises on her black stiletto boots. "Well, she doesn't see it that way. According to her, you left your city, which violates your so-called parole. You're still a wanted man."

She edges by me toward the door and opens it. A cold chill blasts me, and I huddle into myself before she slips out into the midmorning sun.

It takes a minute to shake off the cold, and when I focus on Kai again, he's standing by the fireplace. I didn't even hear him move.

"What's wrong?"

He stares into the flames, not looking at me. "You shouldn't have stood up to her. Now she's going to hold a grudge."

"So? Not like I'll see her again anytime soon."

He frowns deeper and whispers, "You never know. It's not a good idea to burn bridges when you don't even know which way you're headed."

I stand, anger burning my gut now. "Well, thanks for that, Yoda. I'll remember it for next time when a woman is pushing you to your limits."

This time, he does look at me. "Sisters always push you to your limits. That's their job."

I head toward the stairs, but he crosses through the living room to stop me from going up to my room. He presses his hand to my stomach, and I can't help but look down at how his big strong fingers curl around me. "We have to pack to leave. Now that she knows where we are, she might come back, or she could have been followed."

I jolt, the idea of leaving this place sinking in. "No, I don't want to go anywhere, and not because I don't like people, but because I love it here."

He steps in closer. "It's my job to keep you safe, and if I say we need to leave, then we need to leave."

I grit my teeth and pull away to go upstairs. If he wants me to leave, then he can come pack my shit himself. As far as I'm concerned, they can bury me in this cabin.

Once I'm settled in my warm bed, watching the snow, a book perched against my upturned knees, I realize…I'm happy. Not run around grinning happy but content. For the first time in a long time, I don't feel closed in and confined, like usual.

I stare at the pages a little longer, then close the book, pressing a piece of paper I'd found in a drawer to mark my place between the pages.

The snow is falling faster now, and soon, it'll be a whiteout. There's no way we can go anywhere if we can't see the road in front of us.

Kai bursts into my room, scaring the shit out of me. He's changed into a pair of jeans, an olive-green turtleneck sweater, and heavy boots. "Get dressed. We have to go."

I wave at the window. "You really want to try to leave in that?"

His eyes shift to the door, and he pauses. "Fuck. I forgot it was snowing."

"Which means people are unlikely to follow us up here."

He sits on the side of my bed, his heavy weight pulling me toward him as the bed mattress curves. "If not now, then when the snow lets up, or in the morning, whichever is first."

I swallow an argument. At this point, it seems useless since he won't listen anyway.

"Why do we have to leave? I like it here."

He looks me in the eye this time, his jaw tense. "You'll like somewhere better, especially if you get to see it alive."

Is there a point in arguing with him anymore? Not like he's going to suddenly change his mind and see my side of things.

I settle in the bed, knowing I only have a few more hours to enjoy this snowy paradise.

## 13

## KAI

The snow stopped in the early hours of the morning, and I watched it taper off and die. Some part of me wanted it to continue, to give Rose a bit more time in this place where she seems at peace. Of course, fate has other plans, the bitch.

I've been dressed for hours and dreading the moment I have to wake her and tell her we're leaving. Her room is dark as I creep inside, and something in my chest squeezes at the fact that she didn't lock the door this time. I also love that she's sleeping soundly, no nightmares, even with the unexpected visitor.

I gently shake her shoulder, but she only rolls over, tugging the covers to give me a glimpse of her white lace panties and a T-shirt riding up her back.

Fucking hell.

After I get control of myself, fighting the urge to lean down and leave one solid bite mark right on the glorious curve of her hip, I shake her one more time. "Rose. Wake up, you need to wake up."

She fans her hand at me, missing my arms completely. "Go away." Her muffled reply comes from the blanket hoard she's amassed under her chin.

"Rose, if you don't get up now, I'm going to toss you out in the snow to make sure you're good and awake."

She pops one eye open, closes it, and then shifts again, threading the covers between her thighs, and damn if I don't wish that was my own leg or my cock.

"Rose." I sit on the side of the bed and shake it. "Wake up, Rose. We have to leave. The snow stopped a while ago, and I don't trust my sister not to have a strike team on the way already."

This time, she rolls to face me with a glare. "Why would she do that?"

"My sister is a political animal. She will stop at nothing to be the best."

"How do you know? Maybe she's grown up."

I grit my teeth and drag the covers off her body. She fumbles for them as I throw them to the floor. "Because nothing less than perfection is enough for my sister. I learned that lesson years ago."

Her eyes are bright now, fixed on me. "Oh, how so?"

I reach down and grab her by the bicep to sit her up. Her blonde hair flies around her face, and I resist the sweet curve of her breasts against the side of my hand. "Not something I'll go into right now. What if we make a deal? You get up, and once we are safe again, I'll tell you about the time my sister broke my leg for me."

Her eyes go wide. "She what?"

"Nope, not doing anything until you get moving."

Finally, she shuffles onto the bed. I toss a pair of jeans and a sweater at her face, but she doesn't catch them, just lets them fall to her lap and then slip to the floor. "Clothes," I prompt.

I turn my back, hoping she'll change quickly, so I don't get the urge to push her back into the bed and stay a bit longer.

While she's changing, I open the dresser drawers and start pulling out her clothing.

"Hey." Her voice is still scratchy and deep from slumber. "Stop it. Don't pack my stuff. I can do it when I'm ready."

I glance at the clothing still piled at her feet. "When you're ready might not be soon enough. Now, let's go, or I'll drag you out into the cold naked."

She crosses her arms under her breasts and glares. "You wouldn't. Me getting frostbite is not in your job description."

I pull out another drawer and upend it over the suitcase, which forces her out of the bed toward me. "I said stop it. I don't want to leave yet."

She tugs the drawer, and I let her have it since I've already emptied it. Then I move on to the next. "You're right. Frostbite isn't in the job description, so how about this. If you don't get dressed right now, I'll pin you to the wall and dress you myself, and I promise, I'll be nice and slow about it."

The look on her face is pure outrage, so much so that she doesn't lunge at me when I empty the next drawer into the case.

Once the dresser is empty, I stare at the lotions and creams on top. "You have a toiletry bag, or do you want me to just shove this all in together?"

As if coming out of a spell, she lurches toward the dresser and puts her body in front of it. "You aren't listening to me."

"No, but I don't have to listen to you. The reverse isn't true, considering I'm the one here trying to keep us alive."

"Then you go. They're after you. No one wants me anymore."

I spin and drop the suitcase with a dull thud. "You think no one has an interest in you. The only cousin of Valentina Doubeck. I promise you, everyone and their brother would love to get their hands on you so they can ransom you." I let my gaze drop to the swell of her breasts, straining the T-shirt. "Or maybe they will just keep you as a toy, a pretty pet for traveling or something."

She shoves at me, and I'm so surprised I stumble over the suitcase. At the same time, I reach out and grab her by the hips, sending us both off-balance. Once I regain my feet, I'm pressed against her, her curvy body pinned between mine and the wall.

"This is why you don't push people," I warn. It's more of a joke, but tears are shining in her eyes.

"What is it?" I wait for her to answer, but all she does is look away, her body rigid in my hold. As if she's giving up, giving in, and letting me do what I've been dreaming about for months. And I fucking hate it.

I snap my finger in her face and drag her chin forward so I can meet her eyes. "What's wrong? How many times do we have to go over this? I'm not going to hurt you."

She sniffles. "You act like you're going to hurt me. You say you're going to hurt me. How should I know what you will do or won't?"

A burn builds in my chest until I'm pressed into her, meeting her eyes. "You think I'd hurt you, is that it?"

Her eyes are still glimmering, but the hard set of her jaw tells me she doesn't really believe that.

I spin her around and press her face into the cold wall, my hand on the back of her head, my body against the lush curves of her ass. "If I wanted to hurt you, then I'd be in this position. It's so much easier to control someone."

She flails her arms out against the wall, trying to get free, but I press in harder, waiting until she stops moving. When she drops her arms, I ease up, but only enough so that I can lean down and look at her face. "What do you see, with me holding you like this? What makes you so crazy you can't help but fight?"

"Fuck you," she whispers.

I'll take it over dead silence and dead eyes any day. "Fuck me is probably not the best thing to say right now, not in this position."

"Let me go, now," she says, her voice soft and barbed. Each word sharp enough to cut. Too bad I like her a little violent, a little dangerous, and even a little deadly.

"Are you going to get dressed and pack your shit?" I ask, not altogether sure I want to release her yet, even if she agrees. She feels so good against me, so many curves, and tall for a woman, her head reaching just under my chin. The perfect height to bend over something.

She stays silent, and I can't help but admire her determination. If only she weren't exercising it against me.

"Well then, I guess we'll have to stay here until the men with guns surround us and drag us out of here." I dip my head and drag a long inhale of her sweet scent. Damn, she always smells so good. Even sweaty, I can't help but want a taste. I wonder what her sweet pussy will taste like when she's nice and ready for me.

That thought blasts through me, enough that I realize I'm two seconds from grinding into her. I can't do that yet. She's not ready for that, not in this position. At least not until she gives me a little more of that fight I love.

"I'll step back slowly, and you head to bed and grab your clothes."

Her voice is calmer now, louder, easy for me to catch. "And if I don't."

I shift my hips just the tiniest bit, and it's enough to send her flailing all over again. "Don't. Don't do it, please."

I grab her chin and tilt her head back enough to look into both her eyes. "How many times do I have to tell you I won't hurt you? This is me getting your attention. Now get your shit, and let's go."

Another glare, but I step away from her, proud of myself for resisting, at least this time. If we keep this song and dance up, I don't know how much longer I'll be able to.

She shoves at my chest, but I'm ready for it and don't move. "What the fuck is wrong with you? Why do you keep doing that to me? Forcing me into positions you know I hate. You know that makes my skin crawl."

I give her a long look until she starts to calm down. "Maybe it's because I hate seeing that haunted look in your eye. I especially hate when you act like you don't care when I touch you."

I take a step forward, but she retreats until her back touches the wall. But I don't cage her in this time. "I'm tired of seeing that look on your face, Rose, and I'm going to help you get rid of it."

She smirks. "How, by fucking my brains out with your magical dick?"

I catch her chin, tilting it up so I can look at her even though it's probably uncomfortable. Then surprising us both, I lean down and brush my lips across hers gently. A feather-soft caress, there and gone. "No, but when I'm done with you, I promise you will think my dick is magical for real."

She narrows her eyes. "Is that a threat?"

I can still taste her on my lips, and I want more, so much more. "Consider it a warning."

This time, she brings her hand up and slaps my face hard enough to hurt. I wait for her to race out of the room before rubbing the spot that is no doubt already red. I need to go after her, but for now, I'll get her stuff packed. If only to give me a minute because damn, I love when she gets violent with me. Seeing that fight in her eyes turns me on quicker than anything else.

## 14

## ROSE

Kai gives me space, as he should. I can't remember when he started pushing me so hard. It's like everything has become a fight between us. The more time I spend with him, the more I hate it. I don't want to fight with him.

But I'm not yet ready to analyze what I really want to do with him.

I stare out at the snowdrifts bracketing the towering evergreens. This place is so peaceful I can't see myself feeling the same anywhere else. More people, more noise, more things designed to hurt me and break me and take me under it all.

Valentina survived, just like me. She survived, in fact, some of the torture Sal had saved just for her. I can't compare our experiences since no one told me what happened to her that night, but I know he wouldn't rape her. Not the same as me. He made that clear plenty of times. She was never the same as me. The jewel to his crown. He wanted his queen unsullied when he took her to his bed, no matter how much he boasted otherwise.

A chill races down my spine, and I spin to scan the room. If Sal came to haunt me, he's in the wrong fucking place. I'd find his grave and salt the earth before I spent another minute with him, dead or alive.

The sun is rising, casting cotton candy colors over the snowfall. It's beautiful. So beautiful. My thoughts turn to Kai and the wide cut of his shoulders, and how sweat seems to cling to him when he exercises like it refuses to let go.

A knock drags me out of my head and back to the scenery. From this window, I can't see the door, but I can spot a mail truck down the drive a little ways, as if it refused to breach the snow to get any closer. How and why do we have mail? Maybe someone else lived here and forgot to forward the address?

I check the stairs and listen, hearing the sound of a shower from above. Well, he's not about to explore this, so maybe I should. But carefully.

I grab a blanket off the couch and wrap it around my shoulders since I never went back up to put on pants.

At the door, I shout through the wood. "Hello? Who is it?"

A deep voice answers. "Mail delivery, ma'am, for a Kai Aquila? Is he here to sign for it?"

I glance back up the stairs and then at the door. I shouldn't answer, but what if he's waiting on a package, something to help us leave here. "Can you tell me who it's from, please?"

"Valentina Novak."

I wonder why she's sending the package under her maiden name. As far as I knew, she only went by Doubeck now. But maybe she's trying to cover her tracks. There are tons of reasons she'd use that name. The thought of getting something from Valentina is too much to resist. I miss her so much I can't even think about it too hard.

"One second," I call through the door and twist the locks. When the last one flips, the door bursts in, and I find myself staring down the barrel of a gun.

With a sigh, I look up at his face. "Well, you sure went out of your way with this getup. Seriously, you committed to the part, bravo. Did you steal that mail truck, or are you like some mail assassin for hire?"

He scowls at me. "Shut up, bitch. I'm not here for you. Keep your trap shut and sit the fuck down. When I've finished my business with your boyfriend, I'll walk out the door, and you'll never see me again."

I sit on the couch, but he doesn't let me be. Instead, he ties my hands in a weak-ass knot, then loops it around the wooden leg of the coffee table. "You told me you don't want to hurt me, so what's the point of tying me up?"

He holds the gun up, exploring the first floor, checking for Kai or traps. Who knows. "I'm not a complete moron. You could come at me any second to save him. I don't need you interfering."

I catch the twitch of movement above and let the blanket slide off my shoulders. "Well, since he is my entertainment, maybe you could come over here and help a girl out."

His eyes dip to my boobs, outlined by the T-shirt, then down to my underwear and bare thighs. "No offense, lady, but you're too fat for me."

I flinch and scowl. "Well, fuck you too, dick face."

Insulting him seems to work better than propositioning him. He spins and stalks toward me. "What did you say, bitch?"

I clear my throat and take a deep breath as if I'm about to give a performance. "I said, fuck you too…"

I don't get the rest out before Kai comes up behind the mailman and drags him down by the throat. There's a scuffle, and I wiggle my wrists in the bindings until I get free. It doesn't matter, though. Kai already has the guy's gun, and he strips the rope he used on me to tie him up.

When he tosses him into the chair, I scramble out of the way behind Kai. It takes me a minute to realize he's only wearing a towel, and good lord, every time I think he looks good without clothes, it's like God needs to remind me.

The man struggles with the rope, and Kai just stares at him. "Nice to see you again. Ike, is it? Or Ivan, maybe. I get all you boys mixed up."

Kai turns to me, and something about his smile is off. It's almost…feral. "You'd think their parents would learn to stop reproducing. Am I right? Considering how many assholes they keep making."

I nod dumbly, unsure what role I'm playing in this little scenario. Kai stares down at my legs and then hands me the blanket. "For the record, I think you are perfect."

Well shit. I swallow hard, unable to speak after that declaration. So he heard the guy call me fat.

Kai sits on the coffee table, his towel spreading open so he can brace his arms on his knees, his hands folded. "What are you doing here?"

The man, looking almost serene, stares Kai down, not speaking.

I clutch the blanket around me tighter, watching them both. I should be scared, right? Terrified. Not only is this man a stranger, but I also propositioned him like I'd actually go through with it. It's something I might have done…before. A tiny flare of hope kindles in my chest, and I can't let it go. I want to breathe air on it, feed it, let it grow some more, but I don't know how.

Kai's voice drags me back to the questioning. "Did you get tired of waiting around for one of your brothers to take over after Sal's death?"

It hits me. This man is one of Sal's brothers. I freeze, barely breathing, studying his face. It is. He has the same greaseball haircut and extended forehead. A Neanderthal in training is what I used to call Sal. His brother has the same look.

I step forward, and Kai leans away. The man shifts his gaze to me, clearly not expecting anything.

I reach and hit him hard enough to jar my knuckles and shoot pain into my fingers and wrists.

The man flops back against the chair, and I leave a mark on his cheek. Kai sweeps in behind me and leads me to the kitchen. I stand there glaring at the man while Kai fishes out a dishrag and some ice for my hand. "Here, hold this."

To his credit, he didn't ask me why I hit him or why I'm imagining shoving a knife in his chest... the same way...

I pull my thoughts from the past and look at Kai. Water droplets still cling to his neck as if he'd barely had time to dry himself before running to my rescue. "You okay?"

I nod. "Let's just find out what he wants so we can get rid of him."

He raises one dark eyebrow, his lips turned up in a smirk. "Get rid of him?"

I shrug. "What of it? I want to put a bullet in his brain so he can rot in hell with his brother."

Kai turns and grabs the gun off the refrigerator and then sweeps up the man's gun off the floor where he'd dropped it in the scuffle. I stare at both the guns and look at Kai.

He gives me an exaggerated sigh and hands me his nine mill. "Do you know how to use this?"

"Pull the trigger."

He swears softly and guides my fingers to hold the weapon. "Hold it like this, and then you flip this safety off. Don't pull the trigger. Squeeze it. Not likely you'll miss at this range, but if you do, just try again."

The man in the chair starts struggling. "What, you're going to let this bitch shoot me, for real?"

Kai sits on the coffee table again, his dark hair wet and slicked back, his eyes bright. His sharp smile is back, and I love seeing it directed at someone who is not me. "Sure, you did call her fat after all."

The guy looks at me, where I'm holding the gun loosely in my hand. "I didn't mean nothing by it, honest. You're real pretty, just not my type."

I take a step forward and sweep my hair off my face. "Do you recognize me?"

He shakes his head. "No, should I? Do you want me to?"

Sal and his goddamn brothers hurt so many people, and they don't even remember they've done it or the faces of their victims. I'd seen Sal's brothers that night. They egged him on as he hurt me. And he doesn't even have the decency to remember my face.

Tears burn at my eyes. My throat burns. Everything in me burns. I'm so angry my hands shake as I raise the gun to sight down the barrel.

"Come on, you're going to get pissy because I can't remember your name? I meet a lot of chicks."

I glance at Kai, who rolls his eyes. "Yeah, sure you do. Tell me this, why are you here?"

This time, the playful, flirty tone is gone as he studies Kai. "I brought a package."

"And? How did you find us here?"

"The address."

I realize he's playing games, and no doubt Kai figured it out earlier. He seems in his element here, staring down his enemy while trying to get information. It makes me wonder what tactics he'd use on me to get information if he needed it.

The thought makes me hot, and I take a step backward to search for the package he mentions. I scan the address and hand it to Kai. "Is that the penthouse address?"

Kai nods. "I'll have to let Adrian know. But they are secure. No one can get to them and survive, which is why this dickwad went after me."

He kicks the man in the shin and leans over to look at him. "You come here to get me to tell you how to bring down Adrian? I promise it's not going to happen. Not in this lifetime or any other."

I keep my eyes on Kai, waiting for the moment he tells me I can shoot this guy. The man turns to look at me this time. "Oh, you know, maybe I do remember you. The Novak orphan, right?" His smile splinters in my vision into the same man who sneered down at me that night. "I remember now. You were plumper then, and if I remember correctly, you were asking for it."

## 15

## KAI

*I* lean back and brace my hands and the gun against the coffee table. No use in getting splattered with blood when she shoots this idiot in the face.

I wait, shifting my eyes to her, watching her face. She might not be shooting at me, but watching her still gives me the same little thrill. Seeing her defend herself is even sexier than lingerie.

I look at Sal's brother again. He's definitely one of them, but I can't remember which. One of the nobodies, of course, relegated to hooker duty at the family casinos. He won't ever amount to much, and I doubt his family will miss him when he's gone. Which begs the question? Why did he come here seeking a premature death?

I peek at Rose from the corner of my eye. Her hands shake slightly, but she keeps the gun steady. As I look at the man again, I can't help but think of how tired I am of cleaning up dead bodies. Someone else gets to handle it from now on. Maybe Alexie would appreciate the nuances of disposal. Either way, I'd do it for her, just like I did with Sal and Valentina's father. No one on the planet would find either of them.

I'd hide a million bodies if those deaths gave her some peace. Which is why I'm not asking her to wait, to hold out until I get some answers. Well, not until her hands start to shake so badly I fear getting shot in the leg.

I stand and cup the top of the gun to gently lower it. "How about we see if we can get some answers first? I promise, it will be messy and painful, so you'll get to watch the bastard scream."

She nods, sniffing like I'd just offered her an ice cream cone to cheer her up. She lowers the gun and sits on the couch while I take up my spot again. "Looks like you get a reprieve, buddy. So do you want to answer my questions to save yourself some torture?"

He shakes his head, but he's paler now. At least he knows I'm good at this shit. If I want answers, there's nothing he can do to keep them from me short of dying. It wouldn't be a great hardship that way either.

"What are you doing here?" I ask him again.

He shakes his head.

"No smart-ass remarks this time, though. We are making steady progress. Can you tell me if someone sent you here?"

Again, another headshake. "All right, how about a stumper of a question...did you come here for me or for her?"

He shifts his gaze between Rose and me, then glances away.

"Yeah, that's what I thought. You see." I lean forward like I'm about to tell him a secret. "No matter what happens, you're going to die here today. You can die in agony soiling yourself, or you can help me out, tell me the truth, and then I'll make it nice and clean with a bullet to your brain."

I nod, hoping he'll nod with me, but he doesn't.

"Hard way it is then. So what's in the box?"

Rose stares at the box behind me on the coffee table. I pick it up and shake it. It doesn't feel heavy at all, so it's definitely not a bomb. I hand it to Rose. "Will you open that for me? Let's see what he brought us."

I watch as she heads into the kitchen, finds a knife, slits open the box, and spreads the flaps. "It's a candy bar."

Her hands shake as she pulls out a king-sized candy bar and a little piece of paper. "It was addressed to you, but this is for me."

I study the shock and joy on her face. "Well, at least it's not a bomb. Did it really come from Valentina?"

Her eyes snap to mine. "You were going to let me open up a bomb?"

I wave toward the box left on the counter. "I shook it first. It wasn't a bomb."

She sits with her treasure and opens the card. Tears shimmer in her eyes, and then she looks at the man. "I'm still going to kill you, even if I'm grateful you brought this."

I turn back to my prisoner. "So where were we? Since we know what's in the box, and you wouldn't have known anyway, you're safe from that question. The others still stand. Why did you come here?"

He shifts in the chair, eyeing her, then me. "I came here to kill you. To try to redeem my family's honor."

"Did your family have honor in the first place is the real question. Anyone who sells children to the highest bidder should be skinned alive." I glance at Rose. "There's an idea. We could skin him for answers." I purposely make it sound like I'd invited her to go camping, something fun for the whole family. I've learned over the years a nonchalant attitude to torture scares the victims even more than the hard-asses.

She wrinkles her nose and shakes her head. "Too messy."

I'm already turning away, and I glance back with a smile. She's not even in on the tricks of torture, but she's making this easy for me. "Oh yeah, so we are back to family honor. So what happened now?"

"You didn't see the videos that went viral? It brought shame to my family. If I kill you, then maybe we can reenter society."

I don't bother hiding my shock. "Someone sent out a viral video, of what?"

He glances away, and I know it's something dark and shameful. Especially to get kicked out of the world's most prestigious criminal organization. Society has funny rules, but they don't appreciate the wrong kind of attention.

I sigh, wanting this asshole out of my house more and more by the second, which leaves only the torture, as promised.

But before I start to run through what would scare him the most, I look at him again. "Wait, how did you know I was here, and how did you know I killed your brother?"

Rose stiffens, and I can barely see her in my peripheral vision, but I know she's listening now.

"It was in a report from the council, from the hearing for Doubeck. You confessed to the killing."

I don't deny it, and I never would, not with Adrian's neck in the noose if I decided to recant. "So, how did you find me then? I'm in the middle of nowhere at an address that doesn't exist."

"The package," he starts.

I shake my head and grab his chin, stilling him. "No, it wasn't because of the package, and if it was, how did you get your hands on it in the first place? No one would have given it to you."

He trembles in my grip, no doubt picking up my nice guy act is gone. When it comes to Adrian's safety, to Valentina's, to Rose's safety, I don't play around. "Try again," I say softly. "Tell me the truth, or you will regret it."

He opens his mouth once, twice, like a fish gasping for air. "It was sent to the council, and I volunteered to retrieve you for the councilwoman."

I grit my teeth, and Rose speaks up from the couch. "This woman has a real thing for you, doesn't she?"

Instead of answering her, I feign attention on our guest. "See, that wasn't so hard. Do you know who told the council where I could be found? Just one little name will save you a world of agony."

He shakes his head, and I point at the fireplace. "Rose, will you grab that poker and warm it up for me a bit."

The man trembles, trying to get up, but I shove him back into the chair. Then I pull his arms forward and take a look at the tattoos swirling up to his elbows. "Sorry, man, this is really going to mess up your ink."

Rose hands me the poker, and I risk a peek at her. She's quiet and seemingly calm, watching me. She doesn't take her seat on the couch again, just stands near my shoulder, a little behind, to keep out of the way.

I turn the poker up so he can see the glowing tip. "Want to try that last question one more time? You were doing so good there. A nice streak to keep you pain-free before you die."

He shakes his head again and starts panting as I lower the poker to his flesh. It hisses as it makes contact, and he screams loud, his body shaking. I rip the poker away, pulling some skin with it. "See, that wasn't so bad," I quip.

Rose leans over and then back again. "That's a smell that's going to stay with me."

I keep my eyes on the man as he swims in and out of consciousness, but I address her. "Are you okay?"

"Sure, why wouldn't I be?"

That answer makes me turn and look at her face. No, she seems fine. Normal, calm even. "Because we're torturing a man in our living room while practically naked."

She glances down at her blanket shroud. "I'm not naked."

It's not what I expect her to linger on, but I don't push since our guest is waking up. "How ya doing? Want to go one more time?"

He shakes his head, tears tracking down his cheeks. "No, please, no."

"You know how to stop this. Tell me who tipped off the council, and I'll just kill you quickly. You won't even feel it before you're dead. Trust me, I've had a lot of practice."

He swallows hard, and I move the poker down to touch him again, but he screams. "Okay, okay. Just stop."

I hand the poker to Rose, who returns it to the fireplace. "Did you have an answer for me?"

He breathes heavily, and I let him take his time. When he catches his breath and settles himself, he says, "It was from another council. Someone ratted you out, saying it would help their career."

I shift on the table, not giving anything away, at least not to this asshole. "Good boy. Now, let's get this wrapped up. We have a helicopter to catch."

His eyes fly wide, and he ping pongs his gaze between us. Rose steps forward and raises her gun again. When her hands shake, I stand and come behind her to steady her grasp. "You don't have to do this. I'm perfectly capable of taking care of this."

"I didn't get to end old man Novak, and I didn't get to punish Sal for what he did to me. I need to do this."

I lean in and whisper, "You don't need to do this. Dead is dead either way. No matter who pulls that trigger, I promise, he'll never be back again."

After a heartbeat, she releases her grip on the weapon, letting me take it. I step toward the man, him begging under his breath.

"Don't bother. This is for her, and I hope when you see your brother in hell, you tell him who sent you."

I pull the trigger with zero remorse.

Behind me, Rose gasps. I spin to make sure she's not about to faint on me, but she just stares at the man and wrinkles her nose. "How do you get brains out of leather?"

# 16

## ROSE

Some distant part of my mind tells me I should be scared. But I just watched Kai shoot a man in the head, and I felt fine about it. Hell, I felt good about it. One more child predator taken out means the children of the world are a tiny bit safer.

What I do regret is not pulling the trigger myself. As Kai handles the mess, I head up to my room and continue packing. I don't want to leave, but now that the serenity of this place has been interrupted, I can't stay here any longer.

The first thing I do is get dressed. I stare at myself in the mirror, not because the man called me fat, but because I wonder what Kai sees when he looks at me. Then I remember the scars, so much of my skin flawed and flayed his view. The rational part of my brain tells me he has seen it all before since he's the one who got me out of the house that night. The newly awakened part of my brain whispers, *What if he doesn't like what he sees?*

Shutting the voice out of my head, I grab more clothes to add to my suitcase. Then I survey the books that Kai didn't even think about packing. I can't think about them either because none of them will fit as it is.

Once I'm all packed, I drag my heavy suitcase down the stairs. Kai comes from his bedroom with his own suitcase. His hair is wet again. He probably needed another shower after he got rid of Sal's brother.

I'm standing by the door considering disposal methods when Kai reaches me. How did he get rid of the man when several feet of snow was on the ground? "Are you okay?"

I shrug. "I guess? I'm not really sure how I feel. Or if I'm supposed to feel a certain way. Mostly, I feel all right about it."

He only nods, not making me elaborate.

I step out of the way, and he grabs my suitcase as if it is nothing. I layer up and wait for him, staying here in the warm room until he's ready for me to come out.

When he returns, he grabs his own coat and gloves and then leads me outside. The snow reaches my knees, but I ignore it until I spot a snowmobile parked on the edge of the property. Our bags are strapped to the back.

Kai hands me a white helmet and then straddles the machine. I scramble behind him and wrap my arms around his torso. His muscles flex with every movement, and each one sends shivers through me.

He pulls away while I wrestle with the fact something has changed between us. Maybe it's because I feel like he treated me like an equal for the first time. It wasn't him against me. It was us against them.

I give the house one last longing look and then face forward, careful not to press the helmet into Kai's back.

It doesn't take long to reach the edge of the forest and park next to a black SUV. The snow here is plowed, and I climb off the snowmobile and drag the helmet off my head.

Kai grabs our bags and loads them into the back of the SUV. He's silent, and I'm wondering if killing that man had more of an effect on him than he let on. At the time, he seemed so confident and in control. Now he simply looks...tired.

Inside the vehicle, I fasten my seat belt. Kai does the same and then sits, staring at the steering wheel. "Are you sure you're okay?" he asks.

I study him, leaning forward to see the strong slope of his nose and those sharp cheekbones. "I'm fine, but are you okay?"

He grips the steering wheel, worrying the leather until it squeaks under his grasp. "I suppose I'm worried about how that whole thing will make you look at me. Do you think less of me now?"

I clear my throat and smile, something that feels almost foreign to me. "If I recall, you made sure to warn me that you are not a good man. Someone was going to kill that bastard, if not one of us, then likely one of your friends."

He gives me a quizzical look, his brows drawing up. "My friends?"

I grope for their name. "What does Adrian call you guys, His Five? Right?"

He nods absently and then more firmly. "Yes, you're right. One of them would have gotten to him eventually. Men like that don't just fall off the radar and live happily ever after."

I settle in the seat to stare out the windshield. "Nor should they."

His hand on my cheek makes me jolt, and I glance over at him. "What?"

He shakes his head. "Nothing, I just...it's nothing. I wish I could take you home. That we could both go home and be safe."

He seems solemn, and I don't like it. It reminds me of the remote, severe man who nursed me back to health. The one who kept himself behind thick walls. "So if we're not going home, then where are we going?"

I watch as he shifts the car into gear and backs us out of the parking lot. On the snow-covered roads, he leads us out to a clear interstate. "If we can't go home, then we go to my old home, Chicago."

Oh. I wince, but thankfully, he doesn't see it. "Didn't it sound like that man was tipped off by your sister, and you want to go there so she can get her hands on you herself?"

"I don't think my sister did the tipping, and if she did, we would have a confrontation regardless. I'd rather face my problems head-on, not hide from them."

I decide not to point out we've both been hiding for the past week or two. We settle into silence, and I consider what comes next.

A couple of hours into the drive, we stopped for burgers, and I enjoyed the easy silence between us. It's no longer this heady thing threatening to choke me.

Another hour later, we see the signs for the city and start making our way through traffic.

We pull up to a high-rise, and he climbs out first, grabbing the bags. I scramble out after him and follow. He hands the keys off to someone I hope is a valet, and we enter the shiny steel building. I race to get to his side. "Where are we going?"

He points upward with his thumb since his hands are full. I operate the buttons on the elevator, then we step into a small hallway with one door on the end. Two men are standing there, looking very official.

I lean over. "Is the FBI camping out here? Or did we walk into a *Men in Black* movie?"

His lip twitches, but he doesn't give me the smile I'm hoping for. I follow him into the apartment, and the men stay in the hall.

"They're guards. My mother must have sent them after I requested she send a car for our trip."

She puts the suitcase down and waves around the loft-style apartment. The view from the open windows is incredible, and I keep admiring the city gleaming to life around us. "Is this your house?"

He shrugs and then strips off his coat. "It is when I'm in the city. But I spent most of my time with Adrian at the penthouse. There's a room for me there too."

I wonder if there will be room for me when this is all over, or will I be cast out to fend for myself. Although I only met him briefly, Adrian is a very dour man. I can't picture him wanting the random cousin of his wife loitering in his very fancy penthouse.

But I can't think about that right now. "You want to give me the tour?"

He leads me through the space, kitchen, sparse living room, then a bedroom with a huge walk-in closet and adjacent bathroom. There's another room, but he uses it as an office. It takes me a second but then I turn to face him. "There's only one bed."

"No one ever stays here except me, and I've never felt the need to get a guest bed."

I swallow hard, my thoughts scattering like rain on a window. Every time I think I might be ready for something more, the world shoves something in my face to prove me wrong.

Instead of whining about it, I square my shoulders and nod. "I promise not to steal all the covers."

His eyes scan my face, and then he steps forward until only a few inches of space separates us. "You should also mention you snore."

I gasp and bat at his chest. "Fine, I snore, but it's your house with only one bed, so you'll have to deal with it since you brought us here."

He laughs, and I stop and stare. Damn, he's beautiful when he smiles, and his laughter is something else altogether. I don't hear it enough, but that makes sense, considering neither of us has had much to laugh about lately.

His smile slips away. "You don't have to worry. I can sleep on the floor or the chair in my office. It's comfortable."

Something hard sits in my chest, like a rock, making it hard to breathe.

"Sure, that makes sense too, but I feel bad taking your bed when it belongs to you."

He leads me into the closet and clears out some space. "You can unpack your clothes here. I'll be back in a minute. I need to get things set in motion, and then I'll come unpack as well."

I nod, a little bit grateful to be alone with my feelings for a second. Do I want to share a bed with him? Is that what this weight on my chest is? Disappointment?

As I unpack my suitcase, I let the thoughts and doubts roll around in my brain until I want to tilt my head to shake them out of my ears. There's nothing I can do if he's decided he'd rather sleep on the floor than beside me.

It doesn't take long to unpack my things, and then I eye his suitcase but decide not to do his too. He might have a certain way he likes stuff, and I don't want to mess up his system.

I poke around the room, then stare in awe again at the view of the city from the bedroom. Similar to the living room, I don't know how he gets anything done here. There are no curtains, and it's like staring at a photograph.

When he returns, he puts his case on the bed and starts to unpack. I keep my gaze outside. "This is incredible. How do you not just stand here and stare at it all day?"

"Probably because the view from Adrian's penthouse is even better, and it feels more like home to me now. At least it does after all these years of living there."

I turn to watch him again. He unpacks quickly but efficiently as if he's done it a million times, and I suppose he has with all his travel for Adrian.

"So what now?" My heartbeat speeds up, and I sit on the end of the bed, folding my hands in my lap. The covers are cotton and so soft that I resettle so I can rub my fingers over them.

He interrupts me with a little grin as he watches me fondle his bedding. "We prep. The council will see us tomorrow night, but we are expected to show up as the invitation instructs."

I meet his eyes, wondering what kind of ominous shit that means.

It has been a long time since I've been around more than one or two people at a time. The idea of being inside a room full of them, waiting for them to pick apart my flaws and pounce on my weaknesses, is a lot.

Kai is suddenly there, cupping my face, then dragging me into his arms. "You can do this. You've come so far already, and I'll be with you."

It should occur to me to ask him how he knows why panic is suddenly squeezing my chest so tight I can't breathe. But somehow, he does. His strong arms around me give me a little more of myself back, allowing me to breathe through it, and I hope that I won't let him down when the time comes.

## 17

## KAI

My sister's invitation requested we meet the council in black-tie. Because, of course, it did. My sister loves excess almost more than power. In the morning, after a fitful night of sleep, the better part of it spent keeping my distance from a softly snoring Rose, and I took my frustration out in the shower.

It took mere minutes for me to come harder than I have in my life, stroking my cock, thinking of her soft ass cocooning my dick, both of us naked and in my bed. It's a dream because I'm still a wanted man, and she doesn't need the extra scrutiny right now. Also, I'm not entirely sure Adrian wouldn't kill me for it. His orders were to keep Rose safe, not to fuck her, something he'd likely remind me of if it ever happened.

Dammit, I want it to happen so badly. Every time she looks at me from under her lashes, I get hard. Each soft little dig at my expense makes me want to throw her over the nearest table and spank her until that pale skin turns pink from my hand.

I finish cleaning myself up and leave the bathroom in a towel. She's sitting on the end of the bed, eyes wide. She tracks the water drops down my chest, and I swipe them away, enjoying the way she licks her lips.

That's new. Only a few days ago, she'd fight tooth and claw if I came anywhere near her with my erection. Now she's staring at me like she's thirsty, and I'm the last bit of water in the well. "Let me get dressed really fast, and we'll head to the shop. It shouldn't be a long trip. We just need to grab some personal things for you. I already have clothes here."

She doesn't answer, and I leave the closet, tightening my tie as I walk toward her. Her eyes go wide again. This time, she slowly scans me from head to toe. "Am I underdressed right now? It's been a while since I've seen you in a suit."

I tuck a stray blonde hair behind her ear. "No, you're fine like that. I just have a certain image, and I tend to keep it up when I'm here, so no one gets the wrong idea."

She follows me out into the hall to the elevators. "What kind of idea?"

I wink at her. "The idea that it's safe to be around me. That I won't split skulls the second someone steps out of line."

We ride the elevator in silence, and a driver meets us at the curb. It takes no time at all to get to the shop and get her settled on the couch with a hot tea. The owner brings the clothing pieces one by one for us to view. Her eyes stay wide the entire time. She chooses two dresses to try on, and I wait, the owner and her staff leaving the room.

I think she's about to go into one of the dressing rooms, but instead, she stops on the other side of the coffee table and slips her shoes off her feet.

I sit back on the couch, intent on watching whatever the hell she's doing. I don't even care that my cock is pressing uncomfortably into my tailored seam right now.

She wiggles out of her jeans and then dashes her T-shirt off her head in one quick swoop. I can't help but ask, making sure there's no humor in my tone so she doesn't think I'm laughing at her. "What are you doing?"

Once she steps into the dress, all other thoughts of conversation fly out of my head. The champagne silk hugs every one of her curves, giving her an hourglass shape Marilyn Monroe would envy. I swallow, my throat dry.

"Will you zip me up?"

I'm off the couch and at her side in one second flat. I carefully slide the zipper up her back and then step back to watch her spin to face me. "What do you think?"

I stare and stare, and then stare some more. She's exquisite. I blink, remembering she is waiting for an answer. "You look amazing. Stunning. I'm..."

A faint wash of rose hits her cheeks and what I can see of her chest. "Thank you." She calls the owner back in, and they do a quick fitting and bring her shoes to match. We leave several hundred dollars poorer, but I don't even care. I'd buy a hundred dresses if I could watch her shimmy in and out of them over and over. Especially when her breasts shook as she wiggled her hips to get the dress off the curves. Good god, I don't think I'm ever not going to have an erection around her thinking about it now.

We go back to the apartment, and I lead her to the bathroom to get ready. The shop sold some cosmetics she picked up too, and I can't wait to see her all dolled up. She hasn't been since we met, officially at least, and I want to see that sparkle in her eyes.

Somehow, she gets ready faster than I do. Her hair is swept to the side and clipped to stay that way, the dress fits her perfectly, and the shoes make her almost as tall as me.

"So?" She spins.

I swallow hard and head to the dresser in the closet. The top drawer holds a jewelry box containing a special wreath necklace I inherited from my grandmother once upon a time. I slip it around her neck, and the soft sigh she gives me is so worth the effort of waiting at the shop for her to choose this dress.

Once I finish my bow tie and put on my shoes, she gives me a once-over. "You look nice. You should wear tuxedos more often. You make them look good."

I lean down and kiss her cheek, wishing it was her mouth I'd touched. She stares into my eyes, the tension stretching, until the grandfather clock in the living room chimes. "It's time," I whisper. "Are you ready?"

She nods, and I lead her out to the hallway. The guards keep their gazes on their shoes after I give them a shark-like grin. No one touches her. No one so much as looks at her in that dress. No one would be able to look at her and not want her, and I can't handle that right now.

We head to the car and then across town to the upscale museum that serves as the Chicago council's headquarters. When we arrive, I realize I underestimated my sister. The entire Chicago society is here, greeting each other, casting both of us contemptuous looks as they saunter into the building.

Inside the event, the society mills around, and I catch the words open season and curse. She could have warned me that society had opened the season here. The dates are similar but sometimes fall off depending on the time zones back home.

"What, what is it?" she whispers.

I catch the scent of lavender and let it calm me. "It's nothing. My sister just failed to inform me that they'd opened the season already."

"Is that why she wanted you to turn yourself in so badly, brownie points with her society set?"

I shrug and lead her to the bar for a drink, something we both need to mingle with this crowd.

Once fortified, we face the crowd heading into the main ballroom, and I hold out my arm for her. "Ready?"

She clutches her champaign to her chest and allows me to lead her to the line at the door. The attendant takes everyone's names, announcing those present for each new person. It doesn't take long for us to reach the front, and I go first, giving my name to the man. He announces me, which causes a bit of a stir. Rose steps forward and whispers to the man.

He announces her in the same booming voice he used for everyone else. "Rose Barone, only heir to the Barone dynasty, ward of the late Novak dynasty. Now under the protection of the Doubeck family."

She meets me but stares when I don't move. "Rose Barone?"

"I took the name Novak when I was a child and moved in with Valentina and her father. I haven't used that name since I was a little girl. It's about time I take back who I am, don't you think?"

My tongue feels thick in my mouth, and I lead her to the edges of the glittering ballroom. It's still buzzing from her announcement, and I give way too many menacing stares to keep them from approaching us.

"Why is everyone staring at us?" she says after a few moments.

I glare around the room. "Probably because they know I'm a wanted man." It's a lie, but she's been hard enough to get out of the house for months. I don't want to spoil the one night she feels pretty and happy. Not with news that she's an even more coveted jewel than her cousin.

We skirt the ballroom, and I lead her around to find a high-top table to lean on. At least until the council comes to collect us. She clutches me like she's about to drift away on the wind without an anchor.

I study her while she watches the people. Damn, she's so pretty. But a Barone. How had I not seen that coming? I'd researched her when she moved into my safe house, but the only things that came back were Novak's name and assets. The dormant Barone dynasty is rich, richer than Adrian, richer than most of the council. No one can touch her in wealth if she officially claims her family title. It would also make her way too high-bred for the likes of me.

Sure, my family raised the council here, but we were a bunch of mixed-heritage people from two lesser members of their respective families. They loved each other, and that was enough for them. They didn't need the power like my sister does.

It feels like an eternity of warning people off with my eyes until the council attendant comes to collect us.

Rose smooths her dress out. "Nervous?"

I shake my head and extend my arm. "I'm never nervous."

"Ever?"

"Never. It's pointless. Why worry about something you haven't screwed up yet?"

She gapes at me as we follow the attendant through a set of double doors into an antechamber.

On a raised dais sits my sister and the Chicago council, all in chairs like thrones. Leave it to my sister to make herself a queen. "What do we owe the pleasure, big brother?"

The doors close behind us, cutting us off from the crowd's noise. I take a moment to catalog the council present, noting the lack of one of the men who usually sits here. Harvey something. "Can you decide the request without a full panel?" I ask, not wanting to show my hand until we know if she can even help or if she reveals she has already hindered us.

My sister shifts on her throne, her black dress shimmering in the overhead light faintly. "We have a majority here and enough that we won't have a tie. That's all it takes. If Harvey wants to be present for votes, he'll show up to work on time."

I eye my sister, unable to read her mood or the slight shine in her gaze. "Can we have a moment?"

She huffs and waves us out the door like a true queen would.

I march onto the dance floor and turn Rose in my arms. She falls into step perfectly, allowing me to lead. "What is it? Why did we walk in there and back out?"

It's hard to explain to her that I have a bad feeling. "I'm not sure, but I don't trust what's happening right now."

## 18

## ROSE

*I* fall into step with him so easily. It feels like I've been dancing my whole life. He expertly guides me around the floor, something telling me he's done this way more than I have.

"Do you want to tell me what's bothering you?"

His hands tighten on me, but he shakes his head. "I just have a bad feeling about this. Maybe we shouldn't do this. We can leave now and find another safe house."

I eye him, trying to figure out what's got him spooked. I have never seen him rattled like this, and it's starting to scare me. "How about I go get us some drinks?"

When I ease out of his grasp, he lets me go, and I head to the bar to grab a couple of whiskeys. A man approaches before I've even got my drinks.

"Ms. Barone. I'm Teddy Fairworth. We've not been properly introduced, but I thought I'd come over and say hello."

I give him a stiff smile. "Hi."

"I'm surprised to see you here, considering society thought you dead and your family line terminated."

Now, he's caught my attention. I definitely don't like the way he said terminated as if someone planned to take out my family. "What's that supposed to mean?"

He holds his hands up in surrender, sidling close. "Nothing at all. I'm happy to see you're here and unwed by the looks of it." He tips his head toward my hand.

Ew. Perfect, now they all see me as a means to an end, a family name to tie with theirs. I glance over to find Kai, but he's already stalking across the dance floor, his hands in his pockets, the ease of a predator with a scent.

When he reaches me, he tips his face down to kiss me on the cheek. "What's going on here?"

I point at the stranger with the drink in my hand and then give it to Kai. "Teddy, Kai, Kai, Teddy."

They both nod, and then Teddy slips away. I barely take a sip of my drink before Kai has me out on the balcony, up against the wall, his body fitted to mine. "We've been here five minutes, and you're already hunting a husband."

I shove at his chest, anger burning more than the whiskey going down. "That was uncalled for. I was grabbing a drink, and that man came to talk to me all on his own."

He tucks his face into my neck and spins me to face the wall.

Panic rises faster than I can contain it, making me kick out against him. He avoids the sharp point of my heel easily enough. "Calm down, Rose. Calm down. It's me, and you know what I feel like against you by now."

I try to settle the panic in the pit of my stomach. He's right. I know what he feels like against me, and he's not Sal. It's not him trapping me underneath him all over again.

Kai runs his mouth along the side of my neck, sending tingles through my body. "Oh."

"I didn't like that man talking to you. I don't want you talking to any other men. You belong to me."

I gasp as his teeth gently bite into my shoulder. "I don't belong to anyone."

He spins me to face him one more time and wedges his thigh between mine. "We'll see about that, Little Rose. You're mine, and I'm not giving you up that easily."

I hold his biceps, and he trails his mouth down my neck to the swell of my boobs. Everywhere his lips touch, a fire flames bright and hot.

The only other sexual experiences I've had were terrible. I assumed they were all something to endure, but this, this is…I swallow hard, kneading his arms with my hands. "Please."

He smiles against my skin. "Begging already. Looks like your body already knows who it belongs to."

I bang my head back into the wall, trying to break through the haze. Then someone clears their throat, and Kai's sister is standing there in glimmering taffeta, staring us both down. "Sorry to interrupt. I thought we'd continue our conversation."

My face burns hot, but we give her a nod and follow her back into the party, then to the antechamber.

She resumes her seat, and she waves us on like she hasn't got all night. This time, I take the lead. "We want sanctuary from the council here."

"Sanctuary," Selena repeats. "From what exactly?"

I glance at Kai. "The council in our city is on a witch hunt. They want to take out the Doubeck family and anyone connected to them. That includes Kai and me."

The council members whisper between themselves a moment, and then Selena meets my eyes. I'm missing something, but I don't know what. "You can have sanctuary, but Kai cannot. He's already on trial with his own council, and we can't interfere. If he weren't a wanted man, then maybe we could assist. You, however, we can offer protection."

Kai steps up beside me. "Thank you, she'll take it."

I turn and glare at him. "She will not take anything, and you don't speak for me."

Selena wears a little grin when I meet her eyes this time. "Won't you reconsider? Kai is important to me, and I don't want to see him hurt."

This time, she doesn't confer with her fellow council members. "Men like him were made to be hurt. It's his job to take the pain so people like you don't have to. People like his friend Adrian don't have to."

I'm speechless. She'd hang her brother out like that with no protection. Nothing. That settles things for me. She had to be the one who leaked his whereabouts, but what was in it for her?

"What can we do to change your minds?"

She shakes her head once. "Nothing. The decision has been made."

I step closer, putting distance between Kai and me. The plan forms in my mind so fast I can't take it back once the words tumble out. "What if he were my fiancé? Would you give him sanctuary then?"

Her eyes lock on me and then on him. "He's not the marrying kind, or so I hear. He enjoys playing the society playboy a little too much."

It takes everything in me not to stiffen at that implication, but I barrel forward because it's too late to go back now. "You saw it on the balcony. He's my fiancé, and I want him protected as well."

Now, there's something like approval in her eyes, but is it because I'm protecting her brother, or that her brother can inherit everything I have?

She talks to her people again and then looks at me one more time. "You will both be protected."

Then she waves her hand, and we leave. It's mere seconds before she catches up with us. "You better make it official in the next forty-eight hours, or the edict will be rescinded. I got them to be lenient, but joint protection is usually only granted for married spouses."

I nod dumbly, only now considering the implications of what I'd just done. Shit. We have to get married, or he's going to be left for the sharks.

He's not gentle about dragging me out to the car, leaving me stumbling behind in my stupid high heels. Once upon a time, I loved the idea of a party, but that was before. That was the Rose who thought love and sex could be romantic with the right partner.

I'm not such an idiot now.

We both get in the car, and he slams his door hard enough to shake the SUV. I barely open my mouth before he's yelling.

"What the hell was that? That wasn't part of the plan. You can't just take responsibility for me that way and tell everyone we are getting married? Are you out of your mind?"

I swallow the lump in my throat. "It doesn't have to be real. Once you're safe, then we can get a divorce. It doesn't matter."

He stares out the window, his tone softer now. "It matters to me."

My heart aches, and I let the silence stretch, unsure how to fix things. How to make him look at me the way I want him to.

We get to his apartment, and he stalks to the doors, barely waiting for me to get inside. Inside, I strip off my heels and leave them by the door. "Will you talk to me? I'm sorry, okay. I'm sorry I did that, but I don't regret it. Not when it gives me the chance to pay you back for the protection you've given me, to pay you back for saving me."

He faces me, his back to the shimmering city outside. "You don't have to pay me back for that. It's my job."

"I may be a job to you, but you saved me, and while I know I'm absolutely insane most of the time, that meant something to me. I..." I swallow hard and stop speaking before I give too much away. More of myself that I won't be able to get back.

Tears threaten to fall, and I stare at the ceiling, refusing to stand here in front of him, looking like some kind of deranged raccoon. "So what now?"

His eyes find mine, and the look zings through me. Something's changed in the last few seconds, and I'm not experienced enough or smart enough to understand.

He closes the distance between us and lifts me into his arms easily. "Well, I think we should start in the bedroom."

My voice shakes as I stare at him. "The bedroom?"

"Yes, the bedroom. If we have to be a married couple, then I plan to take full advantage of all the perks."

Another owl-eyed stare. "Perks?"

He carries me to the bed and sits me on the edge. Then he reaches under my dress to grab my foot. His strong hands massage my instep, and I don't even bother stifling the moan that breaks loose.

On the other side, I clamp my hand over my mouth because I'm embarrassed but not embarrassed enough to ask him to stop.

"Did that feel good?"

I nod and move my hand to look at him. "What happened? You were screaming at me a minute ago, and now you are here, touching me…" I trail off since I'm not entirely sure what he plans to do here.

He lowers the hem of my gown and strips his jacket and bow tie off. "I realized that I don't care. Whether I belong to you or to Adrian, it doesn't matter. I'll protect you both, no matter what."

"Is that all?" I'm not sold, but he climbs up beside me on the bed, and my heartbeat takes up residence in my ears. "You just give in, just like that?"

He shrugs. "Or maybe I plan to seduce you and keep you in bed for the forty-eight hours until this plan of yours can't continue. How does that sound?"

I feel my heartbeat everywhere now. In my toes, my belly, my face, but mostly in my core. My clit is throbbing, my body yearning to be touched. But my head is screaming to keep him away and not let it happen.

"You could try to, but I'm not sure…"

"Don't worry, Rose. I'm not going to throw you over the bed and fuck you until your cunt memorizes my name."

I blanch at the crass words even as my body heats further. "But…"

"But nothing. Right now, I need you to relax. Breathe, and then we can talk."

I settle beside him and let him thread his arm under my neck to support it. "Okay?"

"Are you breathing?"

I nod and then mumble, "Yes."

"Good. There's one thing you need to know before I touch you."

This time I don't say anything but keep my eyes on him.

"You can't touch me once I start, or I won't be able to resist plowing into you and making you mine for real."

## 19

## KAI

*H*er eyes are wide when I grab the hem of her gown one more time, but now, I toss it up to her waist and bunch it around her hips. She squirms as if she might get up and run away, but I press my hands into her thighs. "No, you're the one who started this. If we were married, I would expect you to let me touch you however I saw fit."

She glares now, her lips pressed into a thin line. "Not any way."

I laugh softly. "No, you're correct, only the ways that make your toes curl and leave you begging me not to get out of bed in the morning."

When she goes silent, I know she's imagining things in her mind. As long as she keeps her fear at bay, I don't plan on stopping. Not tonight. Not when so many men were staring at her, hoping to keep her. Over my dead body.

I explore the curve of her calf, then up to her knee, which makes her jerk and laugh. The higher my fingers trail up her soft thighs, the more she squirms. But not in fear, no, she's tilting her pelvis down as if she can scoot her pussy closer to my hand to close the distance. Which makes me smile. She might be scared, but she wants me so much she's yearning for it.

My fingers reach the lace edge of her panties, but I stop. Keeping my distance, not wanting to scare her with too much too soon. But even now, just this little touch and the maddening scent of her is driving me insane. I fist my cock through my slacks and give it a couple of jerks.

Then I go back to exploring my prize. I trail my fingers down her other thigh and back up. With each pass of my fingers, she eases closer to me on the bed. It won't be much longer until she dumps herself in my lap.

"Relax, Rose. I've got you. I won't do anything you don't like. Trust me."

She snorts as if that's a dumb statement, but I let it go, distracted by the curves and valleys of her body under my fingers.

This time when I reach panties, I run my fingers over the silk, right like the seam of her body to her clit. When I reach it, she jerks, her hips coming off the bed. "Oh."

"Oh?" I peer over the bed at her. "Oh? What does that mean?"

She swallows thickly. "I just didn't expect it to feel that way."

I keep my eyes on her face as I trace my finger over the already wet silk. She lets out a slow moan when I brush her sensitive skin. "You like it, though," I say. She nods, but I don't need confirmation. Her body is screaming at me all the way she likes it.

My dick is starting to hurt, and I'm fearing for my slack seams. I kneel on the floor and reach up to grab the edges of her panties. She lifts her chin to lock eyes with me, and I give her a small smile. "Just exploring you right now. You like it, right?"

She nods frantically and drops her head back onto the bed. I pull the lace away and tuck them into my pocket. Now this is what I've been waiting for. She clamps her thighs together, but I gently ease her open to look at her. Every inch of her skin is flushed pink, and she's soaked, needing to come. Soft blonde curls frame her clit, and I rub my fingers along her damp skin like I did before. She rocks her hips up to meet my hand, so I do it again.

"You are so beautiful like this, spread open like a feast."

"Feast?" she whispers.

I lean forward and fan my breath across her skin, making her shiver. "A feast," I confirm, then dip my head down to get my very first taste of her.

She's just as lovely as I imagined. Her skin is soft and warm, and the taste of her arousal is sweet on my tongue. I lap at her little hole and then make long sweeping licks with the flat of my tongue over her clit.

She's making some kind of noise but using the blanket to muffle it. But all that matters right now is my mouth on her skin. When she settles again, I delve my tongue down inside her, making her clench her thighs around my ears.

I laugh and gently ease her open again. "Relax, love, it was just my tongue. I'm not going to hurt you. In fact, I'm going to make you feel really, really good."

She rubs her fingers over my head and then jerks her hand away as if she can't believe she did it. So I grab her by the wrist and place it on my head. "It's fine."

Then I return to my feast, hiking her thighs over my shoulders to get a better angle. When I suck on her clit, she says my name in a breathy sigh, and I know I'll die hearing that sound.

I keep doing it, loving the way she begins to rock into me, seeking more, even as she wars with herself over wanting it.

It's too much for me not to touch myself. I keep licking her and fumble with my belt buckle to draw me out of the confine of my slacks. Precum slicks across my hand, but I ignore it in favor of one long stroke. "You taste like heaven, Rose."

Her only answer is a heavy panting, her fingers massaging my scalp as if she can't bring herself to push me back into the cradle of her body.

I work my shaft and suck on her clit at the same time, wishing I could stand and push inside her. How tight she'd be as she welcomed my cock. Would she come immediately, or would I have to work her up to it again? I let these things play out in my mind as I pump my hand and suck her little bud.

"Tell me when you're close, Rose," I whisper.

Then she breaks my heart when she says, "Close to what?"

It's enough to make my dick shrivel. I lean up over the bed and stare her in the eye. "You've never touched yourself, never gotten yourself off?"

She shakes her head. "No, it wasn't... I didn't have any interest after..."

We leave that subject alone, and I dip a finger into her core, letting it add more stimulation. "You'll feel it. The pleasure will build, and if you relax into it, I promise, it will feel amazing."

She swallows hard and nods. "I trust you."

I dip my head again and lap at her clit, then alternate short sucking bursts with laps of my tongue. It doesn't take long for her to start rocking into my face again, her hand frantically fluttering on my head as if she wants to push me where she needs me.

"Do it," I whisper. "Show me what you need."

She guides my face to her clit again. "There, just stay there."

This time, I add one finger inside her and suck on her clit until she's pulsing around me, her breathing growing louder, and then when she comes, she whispers my name.

I stand, my cock aching. She takes one look at me but doesn't move. Not even a flinch. "I'm not going to fuck you. Just watch, okay?"

When she nods, I lean over her so I can stare at her still glistening pussy. It takes seconds to trigger my orgasm, and I let it go in thick ropes on her thighs. She watches enrapt until I give myself one last long pump.

I use the soft lining of her gown to clean my cock, but her thighs, I take my time, rubbing my cum into her skin. Branding her with it. Until she's sticky, and I feel satisfied for the first time in months.

She sits up and stares at me, her cheeks flushed, her hair a mess. "Does this mean you're going to marry me and let me keep you safe?"

I gently run my thumb down her cheek, my hand still smelling of her. "No, love. It doesn't. I'm not going to let you throw away your life on me. Not something this important."

Something sparks in her eyes, and she shoves me away to roll off the bed. I twist over to relax on my back, and when she's closed herself in the bathroom, I finally let out a long sigh and clench my jaw. What I told her was true, but I didn't tell her I'd love nothing more than to make her mine forever. She deserves someone so much better. A man who will pamper her and cherish her. She's been through way too much to take anything less.

I rise and strip out of my clothing, climbing into bed in just my underwear. When she exits the bathroom, her face is clean, and she's wearing her old T-shirt. I flip the covers back so she can climb in beside me. She scoots as far as possible when she does, keeping distance between us.

I'm not going to allow that. Not after I just made her come and can still feel the pulse of her under my skin. I haul her against me and wait while she squirms, trying to get away.

"Settle down. Just because I won't marry you doesn't mean I can't want you or touch you."

She sniffs. "Is that all you want, to fuck me, same as every other guy?"

I pause, about to lay into her for her assumption, but I haven't told her the truth, and why should she believe anything else. "Go to sleep, Rose."

"Fuck off," she grumbles.

I rub myself along her backside, and she twists away and out of my grasp again. "No, you don't get to say you don't want me, then keep pushing me like you have been. Either you want to touch me and keep me or you don't touch me at all."

I glare because I don't like ultimatums, and this one sounds pretty final. "You think you can forgo my tongue on your clit forever?"

She rolls over to give me her back again. "When I feel the need, I'll just have to find someone else to handle it."

It takes all my self-control not to claim her right there, take her and make her mine for good. But it would be the end of life as she knows it. I'd never let her go, and she'd hate me for trapping her, the same way she always does when I do the same with her body.

I stare at the ceiling for a long time, wishing things were different, that we were different people. I'd never wanted to be anyone else, but for her, I want to be better. Someone worthy, someone she could need.

When she starts snoring, I climb out of bed and head into my office. With two days of council protection, I can at least check in with Adrian and get a little work done. The council bitch won't breach another council's space to get to me.

For now, for once, I'm safe. Thanks to Rose and her too soft heart.

## 20

## ROSE

When I wake, I roll toward the sunlight, my body feeling tight and pliant at the same time, in a delicious sort of way. I reach out, but Kai isn't beside me. I'm alone, and I'm not sure why that hurts because we've never slept in the same bed before. Never touched the way we did last night.

I close my eyes and remember, causing a heavy pulse to build in my clit. I'd never felt that before either. The pleasure built until I almost felt like I'd break apart. And when I did crack open, it was worth it.

Intent on finding him and apologizing for how I acted afterward, I shove the covers back, quickly brush my teeth, and hunt around the apartment for him. Light gleams off buildings in heavy bands, but I can't peel my eyes away. Until I reach the kitchen and find him shirtless, flipping pancakes onto a plate. Now nothing would induce me not to look.

"Good morning," he says and shoves a cup of coffee across the bar toward me. I take it, wrapping my hands around it, waiting for him to say something. Maybe scold me for being ungrateful, anything.

Instead, he hands me a plate of pancakes and continues making more for himself. I douse them in syrup, keeping my eyes on the broad planes of his back, his muscles shifting with every flip of his spatula. When did making pancakes become so sexy?

I take another bite, watching, waiting for him to finish and sit down with me.

When he does, I turn to face him on the stool. "So, what's going on?"

He raises an eyebrow in question. "What do you mean?"

I wave at the pancakes, him shirtless, the newspaper spread over the other side of the counter.

He only shakes his head like he doesn't understand. "I'm not sure what you mean."

I bite my lip and gaze at the chocolate pancakes on my plate. Maybe he just felt like cooking. It doesn't have to mean anything.

He made it clear last night, but none of this has to mean anything. The problem is, I've spent so much time trying to convince myself that other things that happened to me meant nothing that now, I crave something real. Whatever is between us is real, even if he wants to deny it.

I have no choice but to let him.

Instead of trying to explain, I take a bite of my food and consider my options. He focuses on his own meal, and I find myself with a new awareness of both my body and his.

Every time he moves, I can't help but look. Each shift of his muscles draws my eyes.

Eventually, I give up on breakfast and go back to the bedroom for a quick shower.

It's the most intense shower I've ever taken as I wait to see if he'll join me. Of course, he doesn't. And why would he? I'm nothing to him, not even when I'm trying to save his life.

After the shower, I hunt him down, and I find him in his office already working.

Curious, I circle around to get a look over his shoulder. "What are you doing?"

He snaps his laptop shut and gives me a look. "That is none of your business, young lady." His tone is playful, but a note in his voice tells me his statement is final.

I sit in the small chair next to his desk and watch him for a second. "So what happens now? Are we staying here?"

He shrugs. "If that's what you want. We can enjoy at least another day of my sister's protection, although, if they are around, I haven't heard a word about it."

A part of me wants to argue with him again, but I know it's fruitless. He's made it clear he doesn't want to marry me. I should get out of the chair and go to another room before I say something I'll regret.

It's strange. At the cabin, all I wanted was to be alone. But here, alone feels so very permanent. I explore his house a little bit and then return to his office. This time, he closes his laptop as soon as I walk in.

"Something else," he asks.

I nod. "Yeah, we need to figure out the next steps. I can't just wander around your house waiting for someone to try to kill me, or you, for that matter."

He grins, his eyes sparkling. "To be fair, I doubt a murderer will come to my house to kill me. He'd probably try to do it somewhere less defensible."

I mock shrug. "See, shows you how much I know about trying to murder someone."

I sit back in the chair and watch him. "So...what next?"

The humor bleeds away from his face, and he meets my eyes. "You should go home. Get out of here while you can, before someone realizes..."

He shakes his head and looks down at his laptop.

"Realize what?"

"Nothing, just that you're with me. If they think we are together, you will become an easy target, even worse if they learn who you are."

"If the council is the one trying to kill you, don't you think they'd already know who I am? Especially if they hunted you down specifically when we were hiding away."

"Go home. If you don't do it for yourself, do it for me."

I straighten in the chair, anger burning down my chest in a heavy line. "Oh, you want me to do this for you, so I'll be safe. Rich from the man who flat out refuses to marry me to keep himself safe."

His mouth flops open for a second, and he rubs the back of his neck. "That's different."

"How?"

"It just is. We aren't the same. We don't come from the same world."

Now he's really pissing me off. "Valentina, no doubt, told you what we went through. You know how it ended. How can you say I'm not a part of this world when I was raised in blood and violence? I watched a bomb kill my mother and my aunt. The only relief I felt then was that they went together, and later that they didn't have to see how far my uncle had fallen."

Before he can respond, I shove out of the chair again, leaving it to bang into the desk, and stalk out of the room. The only room I feel comfortable in right now is the bedroom. But even there, the memory of his mouth on my skin is too much to take, especially when I want more than anything for him to do it again.

Since I don't have many choices, I settle in the bed, on the covers, and prop a book open on my knees. If he wants to talk, he can come find me this time.

It's late afternoon when he searches me out, and he places a large glass of water on the side table, then settles on the bed by my feet. "Rose…"

I shake my head, keeping my eyes on the book. "No. I don't want to go through this again. You made it clear I mean enough to you to fuck, but not enough to marry. I get it, it's a guy thing."

"That's not what this is, and you know it."

I still don't look at him until he grabs my face and forces me to meet his eyes. "Will you look at me when we talk, please?"

His hands on my body, even something as trivial as my face, are too much. I want to crawl onto his lap and see what else he can teach me with his sinful fingers. "Oh, don't look at me like that, Rose, or things will get out of hand."

I swallow, my body lighting up, but the fear still flares right along with it. "I don't know if I'm ready for that."

He brushes my cheek. "I know, which is why I'm not, and will not, push you. Not in a million years. It would only confirm what you think about me, and I can't let you see me like those other men. The ones who used you."

I sigh. "I don't feel that way. I really don't. I'm sorry if I made you feel that I did. It's not the same, and I know it."

He moves his thumb in agonizing slow circles down my jaw, then to my neck and shoulder. "Good, because I'd hate to be the same as everyone else. Especially dickbags like them."

I settle forward to give him more to touch, and I'm thankful he does, his hand trailing down my back and then up into my hair, massaging as he goes. It feels so good. I moan before I realize the noise I've made. I swallow hard and meet his eyes. He's staring down at me the same way he was last night, like he wants to eat me whole, and I'll love every second of it.

"What do you want, Kai?"

He stiffens at my use of his name and studies my face. "I want to be safe. I want to do my job in peace without having to worry every minute about some disaster or another. And I want that council bitch dead."

I try to recall him talking about her. "The one who is after you, the one who sent Sal's brother?"

He nods, leaving it there.

I let him continue massaging my shoulders, even leaning forward to touch him. He jerks away so fast I almost topple over on the bed. "You forgot. You can't touch me."

"I didn't realize that was like a forever rule. Like I can't touch you for the rest of your life, or my life?"

His tone is hard. "Ever. I can't control myself around you."

I sit up. "Then don't."

"Don't go there…"

The silence stretches between us, my body yearning for the press of his hands again. "Why are you pushing me away?"

He spins and pins me down with a glare. "What? That's rich coming from the woman who has done nothing but shove me away since we met, sometimes literally."

"You can't use that time against me. I was healing, and I wasn't right yet. I'm still not right, but I can feel I'm on a good path. One that will mean maybe I can have a normal life one day. Without the shadow of those memories looming over me every second."

His eyes soften, and he sits again. "Rose, you are going to fucking kill me."

I frown. "Then marry me. Let me keep you safe like you've kept me safe all this time."

He shakes his head, the softness shifting to a dull glint. "We can't get married. I already told you I won't do that to you. Besides, when I get married, I need certain aspects in a wife, and virginity isn't one of them."

My mouth hangs open as I process his words. "Excuse me. Now I'm not good enough because I'm a virgin, by your definition, by the way, not mine."

He shifts on the bed and stands. "That's it. There's nothing else to say."

He walks out, and I can't stand being in the room a moment longer. I grab my wallet and my shoes and leave the room. Then the apartment. One of the guards trails me outside, but I lose him easily enough. I slip into a hotel with a bar and decide getting absolutely hammered sounds like a way better plan than throwing myself at someone who doesn't want me.

## 21

## KAI

How did I let things get this far and this bad? Every time I open my mouth these days, it's like stupidity pours out where she's concerned.

She cannot understand how much I want to make her mine, how much I want her underneath me, and how beautiful I think she'd look with my cock down her throat. I want her. More than breathing, or eating, or fucking. It's not one thing. It's all of them.

I throw myself back on the bed. The memory of her spreading her thighs, of letting me taste her, is seared there, waiting for the second I close them to rise up and overtake me.

It's hard, but I push the thoughts away. It's stupid, but we can't do it again. I doubt I'll have the control to keep from doing more a second time.

Even last night, I didn't sleep at all for fear one brush of her body against me would be one touch too many for my cobweb control.

I roll up to sit and then head back into my office. I'll give her time to cool off, and then I'll go find her and try to apologize again without shoving my foot into my mouth.

Even after I go through the team's needs, digitally and personally, I still can't get her out of my head. Her scent lingers, and I'm dying trying to resist.

Instead of forcing my focus, I head out into the living room to find her. But she's not there. The kitchen is empty. As is the bedroom, the bathroom, all of it.

I listen, straining my ears for a single sound. But all I hear is the scuffle of the guards outside the door. When I fling the door wide, they all stare at me. The man nearest the door recovers first. "Is there a threat, sir?"

"Did you see my friend? Is she out here?"

They all glance around. "No, it's just us, sir. Your friend went out a little while ago. A guard is with her too."

I nod my thanks, grab some sneakers, and rush toward the elevator. I stab the button a few times, needing it to move, until finally, the doors open.

The ride feels like forever, and I scan the street for her. She doesn't know anyone here, so she can't have gone far. Not without extra money or connections.

But I've learned not to underestimate her. Not when she sets her mind on something.

I jog down the street, scanning faces in the crowds, trying to pick her out of it. It wouldn't be hard for me if she were actually with the people. But no, she wouldn't be. The ball alone the other night was hard enough for her. She'd find somewhere to lay low, to relax, to kill the pain I've caused her.

I glance up at the sign of the hotel and spot the bar through the window. In seconds, I've shoved my way inside, scanning for her blonde hair, the slight slump of her shoulders, anything.

But she's not here.

A bellhop comes over. "Can I help you, sir?"

I shake my head and leave to find another hotel with another bar. It's where I'd go if I were in her shoes.

I check three more nearby hotels, but she's in none of them. Not even a glance. I'd asked the staff, the bartenders, anyone who would speak to me, but no one has seen her, as far as they can tell by my description.

How the fuck can the council call this protection? How can my sister?

My fucking sister.

I dig my phone out of my pocket and dial her number. Of course, it goes straight to voicemail. "Selena. You seem to have a problem keeping your promise. Right now, Rose is missing, and I haven't seen nary a guard or security person from your end. What the fuck kind of protection do you call this?" I hang up, wishing I could throw my phone and watch it shatter to relieve some of the burn in my chest. But it won't help.

On the street again, it's getting dark, and my fear is shifting back and forth between anger and worry. I can't leave her out here all alone, fending for herself, yet that's the exact scenario I've tried to get her to accept. She'd be alone, and I won't have a single say in what she does, who she sees, none of it.

And it will be all my fault.

## 22

## ROSE

The plan forms in my mind the second I walk into the bar and spot all those couples with their heads pressed together. If he doesn't want me to be a virgin, I guess I can take care of that pretty easily.

I get a stool close to the bartender and wait since I don't have any cash. It doesn't take long for a man to wander over and throw himself into the stall next to me. The second he gets within a foot of me, I want to cringe away. The scent of him isn't right. Just the feeling of him near me is enough to send my senses into overdrive.

But I have to think of a plan. So I shift on the stool and meet his gray eyes and try to smile. "Hi."

He gives me a wide grin, toothy, like a wolf. It should've sent me running if I were in my right mind. "Hey there. Can I buy you a drink?"

I duck my chin, going for demure as opposed to repulsed. "That would be great. I'll have whatever you're having."

He signals for the bartender, who brings our round pretty quickly. I practically dive for my drink, needing the alcohol to dull my senses and lead me through this.

Once we are settled in with our drinks, the man leans toward me and extends his hand. "The name's Dan. You are?"

I shake his hand and nod. "My name is Val." It's the first name that pops into my head, and I regret it the second the syllables leave my mouth.

"Val," he says, leaning in again, despite the fact that the bar is pretty quiet.

I hate the fact that he's not Kai. Even more so, I hate the fact that I'm not drunk yet.

His breath tickles my ear when he shifts closer again. "So what are you doing out here all by yourself?"

I try to smile but can't bring myself to let it reach my eyes. "Oh, you know, just want to relax."

In my mind, I'm trying to ramp myself up to asking him to get a room or go back to his place so we can get this over with. Something tells me that if I get pushy, Dan is going to get turned off, which is another quality I absolutely hate about my new friend.

"Oh, same here. I just wanted to take the edge off, you know?" He's almost shouting in my ear now, even though nothing about the bar has changed in the last few minutes. He must have started way before I got here. The idea of letting him touch me, of letting him put his hands on me, is such a turnoff that nausea rolls through me. Shit. He's not going to sleep with me if I puke on him.

I order a couple of waters from the bartender and ease a glass in front of Dan. He takes the hint without a fuss, thankfully. "Thanks," he yells.

It's then that I start to accept that I can't do this. Not even if I wanted to, or for all the drinks in the world. Dan repels me, and he's not Kai. There's no way he can make me feel safe. Not for a second.

"Well, Dan, it's been nice meeting you. I hope you get your edge off."

His eyes go a little wide, and he shifts closer, somehow reading something more in my comment. "I mean, you could come with me to another place, somewhere quieter, maybe?"

I shake my head. "Thanks, Dan, but that's not a good idea. My boyfriend would probably have to murder you afterward, and no one would ever find your body."

His smile slips, and then he starts laughing. "Oh, that's a good one. But really, you have a boyfriend. What are you doing in a bar then?"

I glare at him now, no longer disguising my disgust. "Sometimes people like to have a drink."

"You weren't drinking when I got here, though. Or were you just waiting on some dude to buy you a drink, so you can stiff him when the tab comes due?"

I sit up straighter and fully face him now. "Excuse me?"

"You were flirting with me."

"For a second, I considered flirting with you. For the record, you smell like cheap alcohol, and I'm not going to fuck you for buying me a bottom-shelf glass of scotch. Go home and sober up before you mouth off to someone who wants to hurt you."

He sits down heavily on the stool, and the bartender brings another round. I shove it back toward him. "No thanks, I'm good. Wouldn't want to run up that invisible tab you keep in your head, Dan."

His scowl is nothing compared to Kai's, so I don't flinch when he tries to lay it on me. "Gonna have to look a lot meaner than that to scare me."

Thankfully, he takes the hint and swivels to face the bar, leaving me alone. I leave his scotch untouched and sip on the water I got for myself. He can't add that to his tab, at least.

This was such a bad idea. I don't know what I was thinking.

Dan turns to look at me again, and I shake my head, not even bothering to look at him. "Not going to happen."

He opens his mouth, then snaps it shut, his gaze shifting over my shoulder. Oh, goodie, maybe he found himself another target. I feel a bit guilty for being an asshole to him, but to be fair, he was being an asshole right along with me.

A hand lands on my shoulder, and I'm about to get pissed until I notice the scars on the fingers and trail my eyes up to his face. "Is this your whiskey?" Kai asks.

I nod. "It's really shitty scotch, not whiskey, though."

He shrugs and throws the liquor back. His grimace says he agrees with me. "What are you doing here?" His voice is eerily calm, like the silence before a tornado.

I can't meet his gaze now. "Thought I'd get out of the house for a while, you know, sightsee."

"Sightsee," he echoes. "And your new friend, Dan, over there, were you really going to fuck him?" This tone is not calm. The tornado has touched down, aiming right for me.

"No, not really. I thought it might be a good idea, but then I reconsidered it pretty fast. Besides, he's drunk."

He looks over at Dan trying to hit on another woman. "Doesn't look like he'd care too much."

Kai picks up the abandoned scotch and tosses it back too. "Let's go."

"No, I just got here. I don't want to go back to your apartment to mope around. You're the one who has been pushing me to get out into the world."

He towers over me. "Yeah, out into the world, I didn't think you'd fuck it."

## 23

## KAI

When I find her, I'm so angry I could kill that little man. The only reason he's not dead in the dumpster out back is because he never touched her. If he'd laid one finger on her, I couldn't be held responsible for my actions.

"Let's go," I repeat. It wasn't a request, yet she still sits on the stool. "I'm not joking, Rose."

She glares up at me and then faces forward again. "Every single man in my life has thought he knows what's best for me. You included. And for a long time, I thought I agreed with you. But not this time. This time, you're wrong."

I scan her profile, willing her to look at me. "You really want to talk about this here?"

She spins her stool so hard it hits the stopper, almost jolting her off. "Yes, I want to talk about this here. You refused to talk about it with me at your apartment, so now this is our second option."

I let out a long sigh, trying to dispel some of the anger built up in my chest. I let it go since it won't do me any good here. Not in this situation, or during this conversation, but I'm not successful. Especially since I can still see fucking Dan out of the corner of my eye.

"Please, come with me so we can talk." I try not to drag her off the stool, still hoping she'll come with me without making a scene.

When she keeps ignoring me, I lean in, trapping her between the bar and my arms. "You walk out with me now, or I carry you over my shoulder."

I'm almost proud of her refusal to budge, or I would be if she wasn't using her newfound belligerency against me.

"Fine, you asked for it." I haul her off the stool like she weighs nothing and throw her over my shoulder. Her water goes toppling across the counter, and I throw a $20 bill away from the growing puddle. The bar patrons and the hotel staff watch me carry her out the door without a single word of warning. To be fair, she's not screaming for help. She's got her face pressed into my back as she mutters curses against my T-shirt.

I slap her ass once for good measure when we make it to the sidewalk. "Now, I can carry you all the way back like this, or I can put you down, and we can walk together like grown-ups."

Her answer is muffled by my shirt, so I take a guess and gently put her on her feet. "We can talk when we get home."

She glares, then turns and marches off toward the high-rise. Thankfully, I don't have to chase her down any wrong turns. The guards open the door for us, and she is silent on the elevator ride up to our apartment. I'm quiet, even if my insides are roiling. Anger, betrayal, fear...all of it makes a heady soup that threatens to come up at a moment's notice.

I follow her into the living room and stop beside the couch she throws herself down on. "What the hell were you thinking?"

For a moment, I think she won't answer. I'm about to ask again with a little more heat, but she opens her mouth, then closes it, opens it again. Then lets out a long sigh of frustration. "You're an asshole."

I nod. "Yeah, so what."

"You tell me you don't want to sleep with me, or marry me, that I can't touch you, but you can touch me. How is any of that fair to me?"

I sit down beside her. "Did you miss the part about the orgasms? Women usually like those. Especially when they are one-sided."

She grinds her jaw. "This one doesn't. Did you stop to think about that before you decided to take my panties off and lay your claim on me? I could have been perfectly fine without knowing what an orgasm feels like. Now, I keep thinking about it."

I give her a slow smile, but she glares and shakes her head. "No, don't even think about it. You aren't touching me, and you already said I can't touch you, so...looks like no one is getting any at all."

It's my turn to point out she didn't want anyone within a few feet of her just a little while ago.

Her voice goes shrill, and she storms toward the bedroom. "Well, times have changed, so get it figured out."

I give her a second, then follow her into the bedroom. "If you want to talk about this rationally..."

She rounds on me from her trek toward the bathroom. "Excuse me? I'm not the one who just carried a grown human being out of a hotel bar, for fuck's sake."

"You refused to come with me, and I wasn't about to let Dan have his second shot at you. Who knows, a few more of those awful scotches, and you might have reconsidered."

It's meant to be a joke, but she doesn't laugh. Tears swim in her eyes, and then she turns away in a huff. I move to follow her, but then she returns, and I have to wipe the smile off my face.

She strips her shirt over her head. That helps get rid of the smile, leaving only lust behind. "What...?"

Then she steps out of her pants too. Her bra and panties are next, and I'm already backing toward the door. "Rose..."

She holds her arms out. "Well, this is it? What do you think?"

I scan her head to toe, lingering on the scars from her attack and surgery, memorizing how strong she is, where her waist dips in, and her thighs curve out. "You're beautiful. I've always thought you were beautiful."

She nods, and it seems almost mournful. "Yeah, pretty but not worth the effort, right? Sal said that to me once when he..."

I catch hold of her chin, keeping her mouth closed, her body taut in a line along mine. "You are done speaking his name. It's not doing anything for you to live in the past. Every time you go back there, I have to drag you back out. Understand?" I don't know if she's responding to the bite in my tone or the fact that I have her clamped against me with no space between us.

She whimpers, and it whittles even more of my control. "Now, put your clothes on, and I can make something to eat."

I release her as if she's going to burn me and head straight for the door. Shutting it behind me, I sink to the floor and drag my hard cock out of my pants. I give it one long stroke, thinking about her body and her perfect little pink nipples.

A groan rips out of me before I can stop it. Shame pours into the void of my chest, but I can't bring myself to stop, not when she's making me so damn crazy. At this point, I fear hurting her more than how the sex itself will tie us together.

I want her so badly, and the taste I had of her last night isn't nearly enough to satisfy my craving. How much control am I expected to have here?

I press my lips together to stifle another groan, and shuffling at the door makes me freeze. My hand wrapped around my base, squeezing instead of sliding now, to keep some of the friction going. I need to come so badly. Maybe once I do, I can think straight again. But not if she walks around naked in front of me.

I pump slowly, hoping to keep the sound to a minimum.

There's a bump against the door then… "I can hear you out there. Should I be offended you ran off to stroke yourself when I want to help you with it?"

Her voice and the idea of her listening are too much. I pump my hand faster, working myself up, not caring that I'm about to make a huge mess all over myself. It doesn't matter. Releasing this time bomb is what matters. I have to keep her safe at all costs.

I stroke myself harder, and then her breathy moan hits me. I strain to hear, hoping, praying, needing her to be touching herself too, all at the thought of me doing it. Fucking hell, that's so hot.

"Rose? Are you…?"

"Yes." She sighs. "I never thought about it before, but maybe this will help. Let me stop throwing myself at someone who obviously doesn't want me."

I squeeze my dick, already leaking precum. "This is not the erection of a man who doesn't want you, trust me. I'm trying to keep you safe."

She moans again, and I pump myself faster, not bothering to hide every grunt or groan since she's already listening.

"Come with me, Rose. I want to hear you say my name when you push those fingers inside yourself."

I don't know if she's paying attention to me or not, and the thought grates against me. If she's listening, I want her full attention. I should be the one with my fingers in her pussy, drawing out her release until her thighs tremble.

"Fuck," she whispers, and I swear it's so close, I can hear it in my ear. My orgasm races through my shaft, despite me squeezing to try to hold it off. I pump myself slowly, drawing it out until I can think straight again. When I open my eyes, she's kneeling completely naked next to me.

I almost stop her, but she reaches out to take hold of me anyway. I'm semi-hard now, but I'll be back to raging by looking at her for a few more minutes. "It's softer than I expected," she says.

I can only watch as she explores me, then gently cups my balls in one of her hands. I'm seconds from rolling her over and driving into her right here on the floor. She releases me, and I sag against the wall, the tension now gone out of me.

"Are you okay?" she asks.

I nod, and she gets up and brings me a towel to clean myself up with. Once I'm tucked away again, I go into the bedroom, but she's still completely nude.

A flutter starts in my gut, making my fingers tingle and my cock ache all over again. Shit. Getting off once didn't help take the edge off enough.

I clamp my fists and keep my eyes on her face. "You should get dressed."

She steps forward, and for the first time in my life, I retreat. I fucking retreat from a woman who is going to drive me insane. When she closes the distance, this time, I don't stop her from reaching into my pants, pulling the still semi-hard length of me free, and stroking me gently. She fumbles, but it doesn't matter when she's pressing against me. I can smell her pussy on her fingers, and instead of waiting, I grab her free hand and slide her fingers between my lips to suck her own juices off.

"Did you come?" I ask, staring into her eyes.

She shakes her head, and I haul her up into my arms and then toss her onto the bed. "Well, we can't have that. If I leave you unsatisfied, you might have to go find your new friend, Dan, and have him finish the job."

She laughs and wrinkles her nose, but the laughter dies and turns into a moan as I stroke my hand through her wetness. She's perfect, slick and hot, so ready for me. If only I was willing to cross that line.

I swallow hard when she delves her fingers into my hair, tugging at the short strands.

Okay, I might be willing to cross that line.

## 24

## ROSE

He's saying this is a bad idea, all the while, he pulls me closer, leaning into every caress, every touch. I can't get enough of him, and there's so much more to explore. If he lets me.

I run my nails from his hair, down to his neck, then to his chest to scrape across his nipples through his T-shirt. "Can you take this off?"

He's already ripping it over his head as he mumbles, "I shouldn't take it off. I shouldn't take it off."

His muscles ripple and flex, and I lean up to tug one of his nipples between my teeth.

His hiss cuts right through me, making me wetter by the second. His fingers continue to make patterns on my skin, drawing me in deeper, drowning me in his touch. I still want more.

I shift my hips, so he's cradled at the juncture of my thighs. Even so, he rocks onto his hip, keeping himself from touching me further.

"Don't." I reach for him, but he bats my fingers away. "I'm trying to be the rational one here. You don't want someone like me taking your virginity."

Fine. He wants to be that way. I wiggle under him, forcing him off-balance, so he rests against me, and it takes seconds to strip his boxer briefs and pants down to his ankles. I want this, so maybe I have to prove it to him.

He groans. "Did you really just do that?"

I nod, proud of myself. Until he rolls onto his back, sits up, and slings me belly first across his thighs. "I told you to wait."

I peer over my shoulder, not truly believing he is about to do what I think he is. His hand connects with my ass, and for a second, I'm shocked he actually hit me. Then the sting blooms under my skin, creating a warmth that sinks into me, merging with every forbidden fantasy I already have about him.

He watches my face carefully, and I can feel the hard jut of his cock against my hip. He likes doing this as much as I'm enjoying the punishment.

His hand comes down on the opposite side this time. I flinch and then pant as another wave of sheer pleasure rolls through my nerve endings. "What," I try, but my tongue feels like taffy, my body going loose against his legs.

Another stroke, this time at the top of my thighs, where my butt meets my legs. It starts more painful and then blooms like the other swats, finer, sharper. I'm clawing at the bedding to give myself an anchor in the storm. "Please," I whimper, hardly believing that sound came out of me.

"You like that, don't you?" His fingers knead my burning flesh, and for the first time in my life, I let myself go. I let him take control and give me what he knows I need.

When I come back to myself, he's rolled me onto my back and is lying down beside me. I reach out to touch him, but again, he pushes my fingers away. "Where were we before that little punishment?"

I swallow hard and watch him trail a finger over my hard nipple, down to my belly, delving between my thighs. "Ah yes, I think about here."

But I won't let him get away that easily. "You might have been there, but I was doing something else."

"Yes." He grins. "Being a pain in my ass is what you were doing."

I shrug. "You're going to give in because you want me as much as I want you, so why keep fighting."

His eyes go soft as he meets mine. "For you. It's always for you."

I've had enough of *for me, about me, to protect me*. Every day, it's something else. What about him?

I shove his shoulder, and he lies flat, amusement twisting his full lips. But it slips away the second I swing my thighs over his and settle myself against him.

He's up and out of the bed before I have time to tangle in the covers he mussed on the way off.

But I don't give up easily. I chase after him, and he actually runs this time. "Look who is running now," I taunt, having fun despite the swirl of terror in my gut.

He stops, making me run right into his arm. "Did you say, look who's running now?" There's an edge to his tone that history tells me I should fear, but I don't, not when it comes from him because I know I'm safe.

I swallow the lump building in my throat and nod. "You did run from me."

His eyes go dark as he stares down into mine. "Well, you pushed me to my limit. Are you happy?"

I'm about to make some smart-ass remark when he hauls me up into his arms, walks me to the wall, and traps me against it. The panic flares bright but dies just as quickly.

"I'm safe," I whisper.

There's something in his eyes as he echoes me, and I nod, agreeing, for me, or him, or both of us. I can be what he needs. I want to be what he needs if only he'll let me in far enough to know what that is.

He presses into my core, and I rock back against him, using the wall as leverage. This feels good, not too bad, and each pass of his cock against my clit makes me squeeze myself tighter around him.

I want more, so I lean in and bite his bottom lip gently. He counters, pulling away and delving into my mouth with his tongue. It's a wet, sloppy kiss with grinding teeth, and I don't care because it's him, and he tastes like I imagined. All those times, I thought about kissing him properly and never had the guts to do it.

"You're going to kill me," he whispers against my swollen mouth.

"Only if you want me to," I say, letting him sink to the floor, carrying me with him. I end up straddling his lap, the hard length of him trapped between us.

His hands shake, and I capture them in mine, pulling them to my lips. He whispers so softly I can barely hear. "I'm scared."

I pull myself up, balancing on my knees on either side of him until his blunt end spreads me open. A burn pokes at old wounds for just a second, and then it's gone, leaving nothing but the stretch of him filling me.

I move slowly, sinking down on him inch by blissful inch. He wraps his hands around me again, holding me close. I tip his chin up so I can stare into his eyes. "Stay with me."

The look in his eyes is the same one I used to get...I shove those thoughts out of my head and focus on him, only him.

When I'm flush with his body, I stop, wrapping my legs around him, holding myself there. He stares into my eyes, and I give him a tremulous smile. "I'm not sure what to do now."

He rocks forward, causing a friction and sending shock waves through me. "Oh," I whisper.

His wide eyes match mine, a look of awe between us.

I swallow, afraid to move or even twitch for fear the sensation will be too much and I'll have to stop.

He trails his fingers down to my ass, cupping the cheeks. "Perfect," he murmurs against my lips. I test the movement, using my abs to pull myself forward, sliding him inside me, out or in, I can't really tell, but it feels so good I press my forehead into his.

"This is..."

"I know," he says. "I'm sorry I made you wait."

I shake my head because none of that matters right now. The only thing that matters is the way he feels pressed into me and the tense of his muscles every time I move. The way his fingers keep digging into my hips like he wants to do more than let me lead.

"What do you need?" It's a strange question because I'm not even sure what I need right now.

He shifts his legs from underneath my ass and rolls me flat to my back. I let him cover me in the warmth of his weight, waiting for our bodies to realign. "You are so perfect."

I smile and thread my fingers into his hair. "You're pretty great too."

He chuckles, then slides his hips forward. This is an entirely new sensation, so much more than the first. I feel so full, stuffed by him.

All I can do is hold on to his shoulders and trust he knows what will work. He slides forward again, my hips slipping across the floor, a powerful thrust I can feel so deep inside me, but the base of him hits my clit just right. "Oh, do that again."

He grins, all the fear gone from his eyes. He's with me now. Just me. "Hold on to me then."

I reach up and anchor my hands around his neck and let him start a slow deep pound into my body. At first, memories rear up, but I bury my face into his neck, letting his scent anchor me as much as my hold does. "Yes," I whisper.

Then once it starts, I can't stop it. He's crashing against my clit, drawing my orgasm tighter and tighter inside me. "Yes, yes, yes, yes, yes, yes, yesyesyesyesyes."

Until my body shatters into a million pieces only held together by his body along mine. When I come back to myself, my arms are Jell-O, and my back burns from the floor. It takes me a second to realize he's not finished. He sits back on his calves so he can stare down at where our bodies join, but now, he's thrusting just his head in and out of me, teasing me with it, and also himself.

His grip tightens, and he jerks himself from my body, pumping his shaft until thick jets of cum coat my belly and my breasts. Then he eases over, laying himself on top of me, not even caring about the mess.

It feels good. My body hums with the heavy pulse in my core. I feel complete for the first time in my life. Not in a *he completes me* kind of way, but like for once, my battered body did what it was supposed to do, and I let myself go along for the awesome ride.

I hold his head against my chest, breathing heavily until he gently eases upright and brings me with him. "Come on, shower time."

I want to crawl in bed and sleep for a week, but he doesn't let me lie back down. Instead, he pulls me to my feet, herding me into the shower and washing every inch of my skin from head to toe.

Afterward, he dries me off just as carefully, and we both climb into bed. I don't even know what time it is, but I drift off in the curve of his arm, and it's a dreamless, blissful sleep.

## 25

## KAI

As she sleeps beside me, I obsessively recall how her body feels around mine and how she drags me into her orbit so we can crash and burn together. I listen to her soft snoring, waiting for the moment her eyes flutter open, and I can take her all over again. This time in every single way I've imagined. All this time, I've held myself back, but now, she's mine, and I don't intend to let her go again.

I trace her cheekbone with my finger, trying to memorize every line of her face. The second her eyes open and lock on mine, I gently roll her to her back and sit on my weight between her thighs. She welcomes me, spreading farther to give my hips room. "Have you been watching me sleep? That's kind of creepy."

Gently, I nip her chin with my teeth. "I couldn't sleep, but I could stare at you all day. Seemed like an easy compromise."

"Hmm...say that tomorrow when you want to stay in bed all day."

I arch my body into hers. "Oh, I don't need an excuse to stay in bed all day. All I need is you here with me."

A smile tugs at the corner of her mouth, and I'm mesmerized as it grows. "You say that now, but at some point, we'll need to shower and eat. You know, the usual things. I'm rather fond of actual meals now that I can have them regularly."

I hike her legs around my hips and focus on sliding my length along her already wet seam. "Hmm...it's like you were waiting for me too. So very wet for having just woken up."

"Maybe it was a good dream."

I catch her bottom lip between my teeth this time and then lick away the hurt. "Or maybe you get wet for me so fast because you know what I'm about to do for you."

She threads her fingers into my hair and down the back of my neck. Every part of me lights up under her fingertips. "You'll have to remind me, I think."

I hold on to her thighs as I line our bodies up and slowly feed myself inside her. She stares down between us, as I do too, watching as we join. I can't get enough of her. Her pussy grips me so tightly I can barely keep my control when I'm all the way inside her.

"How does that feel?"

She nods, still watching my cock slide in and out of her slowly. I arch my hips upward to change the angle, and she sucks in a breath, her eyes flashing to mine. "Oh, that's good."

"There are a million different ways. We can explore every one and repeat your favorites."

She licks her lips and then sucks on the bottom one, her neck arching as she throws her head back. "Oh..."

I love listening to her pleasure—every moan, every whimper, every sigh. All of it.

I'm torn between staring at her glistening cunt squeezing me or the stark pleasure written on her face. In the end, I keep going back and forth, watching her for clues, using what she's giving me to make it even better for her.

"You are so beautiful like this, completely lost to sensation," I whisper. Settling my chest against hers, I tuck my elbows under her arms. It feels good to have her naked skin against mine, every inch available for me to touch and kiss and lick.

I nibble on the soft curve of her breast and dip down to tug on her nipple. She arches into me, changing the angle again, and I gasp trailing the motion until I too am drawn into it. She keeps shifting her hips down and then up, and I match her rhythm, giving her the stimulation she needs. Until I delve my hand between our bodies and circle her little bud with my fingertips. She's wet here too. When I speed up my hand, she starts breathing faster, but it's not enough for me. I want her panting, moaning, screaming my name as she comes.

I move her legs forward and sit back on my heels, then shift inside her again, but this time, I have free access to her clit, giving her all the stimulation she needs.

And she doesn't need much. In seconds, she's clawing at the bedding, trying to get closer to me, scooting her ass against my knees.

I speed up my fingers, totally focused on her. "Are you about to come for me, wildcat? Do it. I want to feel you let go."

She pants, lifting her head from the pillow, fighting for her release, and then she shudders, her legs trembling, her thighs clamping as she comes hard. I pump into her until she relaxes, then I pull myself from her soft pussy and pump the release onto her belly. It's not the safest method, but I don't want anything between us.

When the last of my cum marks her skin, something eases inside me, making it easier to breathe. I climb off the bed and grab a washcloth to clean her skin, then my own. As I climb back in bed beside her, she stares, her eyes tracking my movement until I settle beside her, facing her so I can look into her eyes. "Are you okay?"

"Yes, are you?"

I nod. "I think I'm good. I might already be getting hard again, but otherwise, yeah, good."

She chuckles and scoots closer to wind her legs with mine. "I don't mind this sort of touching. It's the grabbing, the pulling, the groping that I hate. You've been both rough and tender with me, and I haven't had a moment's regret."

I lean forward and kiss her gently, savoring the way her lips feel against mine. "Good because you're stuck with me now."

Tangling the covers between us, she rolls over, her back to my front. It's not the same as when I pin her to the wall, but it's a pretty close second. Maybe because she's not trapped with no escape? Either way, I keep my arm loose, easy on her waist, so she knows she can get up anytime she needs. I don't mind the bare globes of her ass pressing into my dick, though, not one bit.

Her voice is soft and sleepy when she speaks again. "Why do you come on my stomach like that?"

I nip her ear gently and kiss the curve of her neck. "Because I doubt you're in the market for any children right now. But trust me, coming inside you, feeling my release run down your thighs, is a decadent pleasure I plan to have very soon. We just need to figure out the logistics first."

She nods, settling her hand under her cheek and then smacking her lips together. "That's fine."

If she were more awake, I'd spank her for her half-hearted response to me coming inside her. When it's time, I hope she loves it too.

I kiss her neck again and wrap my arm a bit tighter, so I can feel the bottom of her breasts against my forearm. She makes another sleepy sound, and I can only watch as sleep claims her again.

I want to pull her harder into me, slide into her from behind, just like this and fuck her awake. Let her wake up coming around me. The idea sticks in my head, and I let it stay there, something for us to do together soon, if she would like it.

My chest feels tight as I watch her sleep. There are a hundred things I want to say. None of them are important, yet all of them are clamoring for me to speak the words so they are out of my head. Even purging them from my mind won't help. I still feel them. Every little thing she does that makes my heart ache painfully in my chest will still be there. That's not something I can push down or strip away.

I trace my lips against her shoulder blade, thinking. We've never really talked about feelings before. I'm not one of those guys who shares that sort of thing, but with her, I want her to know that she keeps my heart beating. Her words, her scent, her anger, and the violence I catch in her eyes keep my heart suspended in my chest, but it belongs to her. I'm just not sure she is ready to hear that truth yet, nor am I ready to speak it.

Her voice cuts through my thoughts. "You know, I'm not a virgin anymore, by your definition now, so we can get married, and you can be safe."

The idea that she only wants to be with me, marry me, to keep me safe both angers and humbles me. I give her another kiss. "Go to sleep. We can talk about it tomorrow if you want."

She rolls, blinking the sleep from her eyes, the exact thing I just told her not to do. "What? Really? You've reconsidered now that we've had sex. That's all it took?"

I don't need to remind her that us sleeping together was no small thing for either of us.

"Go to sleep. We can talk about it properly tomorrow. We are both too tired to be rational right now. Besides, if you start talking to me, I'm going to have to fuck you again, and I think you might be too sore for that."

To my surprise, she doesn't argue. She rolls again, resettles against me, and does as she's told.

I don't have the heart to tell her that we'll never be safe as long as that council bitch is alive.

## 26

# ROSE

In the morning, he's the first thing I reach for. I slide my hands through the warm sheets and find nothing but an empty indent where he fell asleep beside me after the last time he took me.

Heat burns up my neck and into my cheeks at the thought. Not because I'm ashamed, but because I hadn't imagined sex could be so...imaginative. And Kai has a very, very good imagination. There are muscles in my body that are sore I didn't even realize were there.

I roll over, searching for him, and freeze when I find him sitting beside the edge of the bed, on the floor. "Are you okay?"

He nods, his eyes solemn.

I start to get up, throwing off the tangled sheets. "What is it? Is everyone all right? Valentina?"

He slides one hand across the bed and takes mine. When he speaks, his voice is whisper-soft, as if he can't get the words out. "Everyone is fine. Nothing is wrong. Calm down."

I don't appreciate him telling me to calm down when he's kneeling at the side of the bed, but I settle back on the pillow and jerk the sheet up to cover my naked skin. His eyes track the movement, but he doesn't comment on it.

There's only one other reason a man kneels on the floor like this, and something strange clogs my throat at the idea. I want this, but not out of obligation or guilt.

Doing it to protect his life is something different. At least that's what I tell myself.

Shit. Now that he's there, not even asking the question yet, I don't think I can do it. "Please, get up. Let's talk about this for a second."

His eyes narrow. "Are you joking? We have been arguing about this very thing for days now. Well, that and sex, but…"

Thankfully, he gets off the floor and slides into bed beside me. Which I realize is a very bad idea the moment his warm hands slide over my bare skin. When he touches me, I can't think straight. Even harder when I catch sight of his completely naked body and feel the evidence of how much he wants me. "What do you want, Rose? I don't want to marry you so I don't ruin your life and you push for it. I decide we should get married, so I can lick between your creamy thighs every day, at least until you get tired of me, and you tell me no and look like you want to bolt."

When he puts it like that… I clear my throat and sit beside him so we aren't touching. The white sheet isn't much of a barrier, but I have to do something, or this will devolve quickly, and nothing will get solved. "It's not that I don't want to marry you. I just don't want you to feel trapped into it. Bound by your circumstances."

"Isn't it the other way around? You are bound by these circumstances just as much as I am. You didn't have to make that deal with the council. You could have left me to rot on my own and protected your own ass."

He reaches for me, and I shake my head, holding him at bay with a hand on his chest. "I don't need protection anymore, not the same way you do."

"You don't think Sal's family will come for you when they learn what truly happened that night."

I jerk my eyes from him and look away. "You think they will come after their son's victim, even if his death is related to someone else's attack. I have no disillusions that Adrian went after Sal because of what he did to Valentina. It has nothing to do with me. He probably knows very little about me, save him helping me medically when I needed it."

He snatches my hand up so fast I can't react before he pulls me into the curve of his shoulder and settles me there. "Adrian knows who you are and what you mean to Valentina, which makes you important to him. He might have killed Sal for her, but I doubt his family will care when it comes to details. They want all of us dead."

I swallow down the guilt, still clogging my throat, unable to admit the last part of my hesitation.

A tiny part of me wants him to agree because he actually cares, not because of some obligation or threat.

After a moment, he whispers one word into my hair, cupping the side of my head to his mouth. "Please."

I can't resist the soft plea in his tone. "Yes. Fine. I'll marry you, but I at least want a dress that won't make me feel like an idiot to wear."

He rolls me over onto my back and settles between my thighs. "Really?"

I nod, and his smile makes my throat tight. Fucking hell, I'm falling in love with him. It hits me like a damn Wylie Coyote anchor. Shit. This won't make things easier when, one day, we must go our separate ways. I know he's only been stuck with me to keep me out of the spotlight while Adrian deals with the threat to him and the council. But, in the short time I've been with him twenty-four seven, I've gotten to know him better. He's smart, so fucking smart, and the way his mind works is fascinating. I don't think a lifetime would be long enough to figure out his every nuance.

Isn't that why people marry, so they can spend a lifetime learning about the person they love?

Except this will be one-sided. Protection for both of us, maybe, and a little fun in the sheets. I doubt after him, I'll be able to find someone who makes me feel as safe or cherished when I'm touched.

While I've been thinking, he plants a kiss on my cheek, climbs out of bed, and enters the closet. "We need to get dressed. I can have your outfit, the lawyer, and a judge here within the hour. Is that too soon?"

Too soon to trap him into a marriage? Probably. Too soon to spend my life with him? No, never.

I swallow hard and roll away so I can get a hold of myself before I climb out of the bed. "Just let me know if you need me to do anything."

He rushes over, kisses my cheek again, and then heads out of the room, calling after him. "You just need to show up."

When he said within an hour, he wasn't kidding. Not an hour later, before I've even had breakfast, two strangers and one creamy silk dress are waiting for me. It takes a minute to put on a little makeup and make the dress look purposeful. I leave my feet bare since I don't have shoes to match, and when I enter the living room, Kai hands me a white rose to carry in front of the severe man standing near the door.

"Ah," he says, his voice like the scratch of tree branches on a windowpane. "Let's get this over with since you didn't seem to want to wait for the proper time."

I lean into Kai, who is dressed impeccably in a black-on-black suit, a white rosebud in his lapel. "You didn't kidnap him, did you?"

He brushes his forehead with mine. "No, but I'll save that idea for next time since he might complain less if he thinks I'll actually hurt him."

We go through the entire spiel, and I try to keep my face neutral and blank as we say our empty vows. He doesn't, each word laced with emotion, and I have to remind myself it's probably an act. He's making sure these people think this is rushed out of love, not necessity.

When it's over, we sign the paperwork, everything is notarized, and Kai opens the door wide. "Get out. I have to fuck my wife to within an inch of her life."

Heat flames my cheeks, and I head into the kitchen to slip the rose into a glass of water. It won't last long, but I've never been given a flower before, so I want to savor it a little longer.

He comes up behind me, cupping my hips back into him before I can turn around.

Sheer panic threads my pulse, shooting it in my face, my neck, my head. I splay my fingers on the cold granite countertop, trying to fight it back, but I still tremble from the onslaught.

"Shhhh," he whispers, pulling me back into his chest but not caging me in, not trapping me. "I'm with you. You're safe."

Those words are enough to help me push the panic aside and return my breathing to normal. Dammit. When can that asshole stop fucking up my life already? I hate that every single day is laced with the memory of Sal, even if I don't want them.

He sinks to his knees and opens the silk tie at my waist to spread the dress open. It drapes off my shoulders as he fingers the edge of my panties. "Let's try something else, shall we?"

I'm nude from the waist down in seconds, my panties stripped away. He lifts me onto the countertop's edge and throws my legs over his shoulders in one smooth move. "Lie back," he orders with an edge to his deep voice.

I do as he requests and ignore the chill of the cold counter underneath me. It's an interesting combination with the hot feel of him wedged between my thighs.

He nibbles from my knee to the sensitive skin at the top of my thighs. "Mmm..."

I reach out and trail my fingers through his hair. Not directing him, but simply wanting to touch him too.

When he licks me from core to clit, I arch off the counter, and he has to hold me down with one strong forearm. "Are you going to wiggle all over the place or let me work?" he says against my already wet flesh.

I swallow thickly and try to keep still. Which is impossible when his teeth graze my clit, and he finds a rhythm with his other. His fingers spear inside me, reminding me how new I am to all this, but his tongue and teeth do wicked things to my clit, rolling it and biting it. It's the tiniest hint of pain that shoves me over the edge of my orgasm.

I can't feel my fingers and toes as the sensations course through me. He stands, sliding my thighs down around his hips now. "Is my bride satisfied?"

Reaching for his lapels, I drag him on top of me for a kiss. He tastes like sex, my pussy, and something that is all him. When his fingers spear into my hair, fisting it at the nape, I'm already wet for him again.

"Fucking hell, what you do to me," he whispers against my cheek. "I'm going to take you over and over. And if you can still walk when I'm done, then I'll continue until you're as bowlegged as a baby deer."

I chuckle, unable to help it. "That doesn't sound very romantic."

It's his turn to laugh. "Oh, it will be when I lick your clit, your cunt, your asshole, all of it. There's not an inch of your body I won't know the taste of, Rose. Can you handle that?"

I swallow hard and nod, unable to describe the war going on inside me at his words.

Fucking hell, I want all of it, but every time he looks at me, I fear he's only here out of obligation, of duty, his promise to Adrian to keep me safe. If this is the only way, then of course, he'd do it. Even *I* know that much about his sense of honor.

I just really hate how much I wish this were real. I swipe at a stray tear and kiss him so he doesn't see. Maybe for a little while, I can pretend.

## 27

## KAI

The apartment is quiet today, or maybe that's the usual noise inside my head staying calm. Being around her and seeing her smile does something to me. She gives me peace in a way that shouldn't be possible after everything I've done.

I head into the kitchen naked and grab some eggs from the refrigerator. I've barely started the coffee when she marches out of the bedroom wrapped in the wrinkled bed sheet. Her hair is a mess, and I've never seen a more beautiful woman.

She grabs some of the cheese off the plate near the stove and nibbles on it, but I see something else I want to taste.

When I spin her to face the countertop, her belly pressed against the edge, she tenses. I don't move, letting her get used to the feel of me behind her pressed against her backside.

I can't pinpoint the moment, but she trusts me. It's imperative that I don't break it. Not just to her but also to me. "Hungry?" I ask against the slope of her neck.

"Mmm...yes, but not for eggs."

She leans into me, and I skim my hand down her front, parting the sheet so I can touch bare skin. "How about some bacon then?"

I lick my lips as she curls her hand back behind my neck to pull me down. "No, it's not the bacon I want either."

With my teeth and my tongue, I mark the ridge of one smooth shoulder, then do the same to the other side. "No bacon then." I'm getting hard with the globes of her ass framing my cock. I lick my lips and gently peel the sheet away from her skin, letting it fall to the floor. "I have an idea?"

She dips her head back against my shoulder to look up at me. "What kind of idea?"

Leaving one hand on her waist, I use the other to turn off the burner and move the pan. "How about we try something new? Well, new to you, no doubt."

There are questions in her eyes but no fear. I can work with that.

I trail one hand over the soft mound of her belly and slip between her thighs. She's already wet, and I give her clit a little swirl with my fingers.

When I bring the other hand to her mouth and slip my thumb between her teeth, she gets the idea and licks it for me. After I slide it free, she can't help but ask the question. "What are you about to do?"

My only answer is a smile, one I know will drive her nuts since it tells her nothing.

Keeping my one hand on her clit, forcing her to pay attention to it now, I trail the other hand down her ass and use my fingers to part her cheeks. "Bend over the counter just a bit for me, wildcat. I promise it will be worth it."

She does as I ask and leans over the counter, careful not to trap my hand against the granite. I slip down, resting my wrist against her thigh.

Every second of stimulation makes her more wet, and I'm dragging my length along her hip as I touch her.

I skim my finger over the little pucker of her asshole, and she tenses, a little gust of air leaving her.

"Relax, I'm not going to fuck you here yet. That will take some time for you to get used to. Consider this an appetizer."

She presses her chest and cheek over the counter, coming up on her tiptoes to give me better access. With the thumb she sucked, I gently ease into her back hole, a tiny bit at a time, all the while moving faster on her clit. "That's it, relax for me," I whisper, keeping my eyes on her face in case it becomes too much for her. "How is that? How does it feel?"

She nods, squeezing both her eyes and her mouth together as if she's trying to stifle her reactions. "Good," she says with a gust of air. "It feels good. Don't stop."

I work my thumb in farther, marveling at how tight it will feel around my cock one day. I'm about ready to explode just watching her take this, so I can't imagine when it's my cock stuffing her fully. "Are you close? Relax into it and breathe for me."

She exhales again, a moan chasing it, and it goes right through me. Fucking hell, she's sexy. Her nails dig into the wrist at her front, and I didn't even realize she'd grabbed me.

"Don't stop," she chants.

I press a kiss to her shoulder blade and work my hands faster, fucking her ass with my thumb while working her clit with my fingers.

She shatters with a soft whine, which rolls into her moaning my name. I swallow hard, shifting so I can keep my aching cock against her. Another few seconds and she squeezes my wrist to stop me from continuing.

I pull away from her and head to the sink to wash my hands. "I'd lick off the juices of your little pussy, but I'm about to make breakfast, so let's keep things sanitary, shall we?"

She stands, grabs the sheet off the floor, and wraps it over her breasts like a towel. "We aren't quite finished here?"

I turn to face her, a grin on my lips, leaning against the sink edge while I dry my hands. "What does that mean?"

Careful of the sheet's trail, she crosses to my side and sinks to her knees at my feet. I swallow hard at the view, the air suddenly hard to breathe. She takes me in hand, dips her head forward, and clamps her mouth around me as far as she can get it.

I reach around to hold the countertop, needing the support. "Shit, Rose."

She rolls her eyes up to look at me and takes another long suck with her mouth, her hand following her lips to my crown and then back again. I dig my fingers into her hair, knowing I'm not going to last long. "A little harder for me."

Like a fucking champ, she added more pull, and then the tiniest graze of her teeth sends me over the edge. She takes that too, swallowing me down, lapping up my cum until my knees feel like they are about to give out.

When she's done, she wipes her mouth with the sheet, and I help her stand. "How was that?"

I kiss her hard, tangling our tongues together. When I let her up for air, she's dazed and unsteady. "Fucking amazing."

A pink flush tints her neck, and she turns to the eggs I'd abandoned in favor of her body. "Let's finish this food so we can eat and then do other more fun things."

I get one last feel of her ass and head into the bedroom for a quick shower. If she cooks, then I'll eat. If she doesn't, then I'll cook and feed her myself.

It doesn't take me long to clean up, not with my mind on her body and when I can get inside her again. When I exit the bedroom, drying my hair with the towel, my boxer briefs on, for now at least, I find her scrambling eggs with a phone pressed to her ear.

My heart stops, and I close the distance in a few strides, snatch the phone from where she's holding it between her head and her neck, and hang it up. "What the hell are you doing?"

She freezes, the spatula raised, the sheet precariously close to falling since I set her off-balance. "What's wrong?"

I wave the phone at her. "Who were you talking to?"

"Valentina. I haven't spoken to her since the cabin, and I wanted to give her an update on things."

I don't let her continue explaining. She trails me as I march to the bedroom, grab the suitcases from the closet, and toss them on the bed. "Start packing."

She hugs the sheet to her chest. "Why? What's going on? I don't want to leave again."

While I'm thinking about it, I switch the phone off and take out the battery. Then swing around and grab clothes to wear and the ones that need to go into the case.

Her hands are cold when she grabs my bicep. "What's going on? Talk to me."

"You called Valentina. We've had a spy in the house for some time. We thought we had gotten rid of her, but we can never be sure. Not to mention anyone can be bugging our phones, or computers, this apartment, all of it."

The confused look she wears shifts, her lips turning down, her gaze heavy. "If you were that worried about it, why didn't you say something?"

I throw clothes in the case and look at her side of the closet. "Because I didn't want to give you even more to worry about when you are just..."

"Just what?"

I stop and swallow hard, meeting her eyes. "When you were just starting not to hate me."

She shakes her head, chasing me into the closet this time. "I never hated you. You piss me off a lot, sure, but I've never hated you."

Nothing I can say will make this all right. We have to leave again, and it's been my fault from the beginning. It's not fair to her. I sit on the end of the bed, abandoning the fistful of clothes I'm holding, letting them slip to the floor. "You can stay here. They only want me. She only wants me."

Rose shuffles to me and sinks down so she can look up at my face. "What about the council here, your sister? They are supposed to be protecting us. That's why we came here and did that whole dog and pony show, to begin with."

My tongue feels thick, and I have to swallow before I can speak again. "Yeah, but there haven't been any calls, any guards, nothing. I'm starting to think my sister can't protect us any more than she can protect herself. Why do you think she was so intent on making an alliance with the council of another powerful city? She's scared of something or someone."

"Can we help her?" she asks, sliding her hand up my thigh to tangle our fingers together.

I snort and look away. "You are too kindhearted for this world. She'd hang you out to dry in a second if it furthered her political ambitions. A guppy can't help a shark, not unless it wants to be food."

She scowls, pulling her hand from mine. "I may be too nice, but that's not something I should be ashamed of or stop doing because everyone else is a dick."

I fold over and cradle my head as she walks out of the room. Awesome. I'm messing things up all around today. I give myself a minute to wallow, then I get up, face the suitcases, and start folding again.

I'm almost done when she comes back into the room, grabs some clothes, and storms back out again. It's not our first argument, or hell, even our second, but those were before when I had to fight her into living, into staying. This time, both of us, and not just her, have to face facts. We are different people, and we see the world differently.

I sit on the edge of the bed again, using the space to fold the clothes even though it doesn't really matter since they are all going in the case anyway. Does Adrian have this same problem? Valentina is one of the sweetest people I've ever met. How does he reconcile her tender heart with his dark one? None of us are deluded enough to think we are kind, or generous, or anything like that. But Valentina and Rose, they aren't the same as us.

It's only a matter of time before they realize we don't deserve them.

## 28

## ROSE

I can hear him throwing things around in the bedroom, mostly grumbling as he shifts the cases and tosses clothes into them. Occasionally, I'll hear a boot and a muttered curse. Once I'm dressed, I resolve to stay out of there, at least until packing is no longer not an option. We'll be leaving whether I like it or not. That's what he hasn't said.

I hate that I don't have a choice and that we can't find somewhere to settle and be safe. I'm barely coming back to myself, and I don't want things to be continually ripped from my grasp.

With him occupied, I sit in the living room, staring out at the view. It truly is stunning. Maybe soon, when things have resolved, we can see his home there. I'm eager to talk to my cousin again, and even more so to live in a place that is mine, ours even. However long I'll get that luxury.

The city sparkles in the midday sun, its shimmer and shine a lie to look at. Seeing the city from this view makes me think it will be warm and beautiful, but I know the second I walk outside, the cold trapped between the high-rises will chill me to the bone. At least that's how it's been recently. Having been nowhere but the Novak mansion, the cabin, and now here for as long as I remember, I don't have much to compare the weather to.

Something thumps against the wall, and I twist around to glare at the door. At this rate, he'd have already packed the entire bedroom into two small suitcases. Seems unlikely. There's one more thump, and I shake my head and sigh, resuming my study of the view. I'm going to miss it most, I think.

A few more seconds of silence brings him out of the bedroom, but I refuse to look at him. Not when he hasn't apologized or said a civil word to me since earlier. And I still haven't gotten breakfast.

"Are you going to ignore me like a child?"

I shrug, not looking, "I don't know. Are you going to continue throwing things around the bedroom like a child?"

With a huff, he loudly does something behind me that makes me look. The suitcases are there, standing in the foyer area of his apartment. "Ask the guards to take these down to the car, please. I'll be out in a moment when I don't feel like I want to strangle you again."

I can only glare at his back when he retreats to the bedroom once more. With a sigh, I heave myself up and head to the door to ask the guards for help, even if we are both capable of carrying our own bags. If only it will give him one less thing to bitch at me about this morning.

Marital bliss can go fuck itself.

I open the door and stare at the empty hall. "Maybe they went on break," I whisper to myself and turn back to the suitcases. It won't take much effort to put them in the hall and direct them when they return.

I'm in the middle of getting the suitcase to slide right on the floor when I feel something cold against my neck. "Oh, well, don't you look pretty," a voice says from behind me, a voice I don't recognize.

I tighten my grip on the suitcase, testing its weight, but it'll be way too heavy to swing around and hit the man. Seems Kai's penchant for overpacking is an even bigger problem than having to lug heavy things into vehicles at the moment.

"You should probably leave," I say, keeping my voice steady. "The last person who held me at gunpoint didn't end up very well."

He presses the gun into my neck harder, digging it in. "I suspect you mean my cousin. Where is he?"

I shrug. "Not sure. He had an unfortunate incident with a fire poker. He's probably grizzly bear food by now. How did you find us?"

He doesn't answer, and I resist the urge to turn and look at him. If you've seen one of Sal's disgusting family members, you've seen them all. And if I look at him and recognize him, I might not be able to resist the urge to attack him. Which might get me killed faster.

I swallow hard, oddly proud of myself, considering how short a time ago I'd been all aggression and no logic.

"You think you're so clever, don't you? But you're not. You and all your kind are worthless wastes of space, only good for fucking and killing," he says, his voice dark and angry.

"Well then, I guess that puts me in my place. Do you mean me, in particular, my family, or women in general?" I resist the urge to quip about his likely inability with women, at least.

The gun digs in at my nape, and I look around for a weapon, anything I can use to get space between him and me. All I need right now is for

Kai to come out of the bedroom and check on me again, or at the very least to make sure I did what he asked and find us.

I rack my brain and can't think of anything. In the hall, with the guards likely incapacitated somewhere, there's nothing I can do to save myself. That's the most chilling thought of all.

I couldn't save myself then either.

"Where is your keeper?" he asks abruptly.

I think hard. If he's here for Kai, maybe I can get away and find help, but I won't leave him to be shot, or worse, while I'm gone.

"Oh, you know, he went out to get some breakfast." It's not my best work, and no one in their right mind would be convinced.

"Well, that's bullshit since I've been outside all morning, then out here after I killed your guards. He never left the apartment." He grabs my arm and spins me to face him, the gun now digging into the side of my neck. "Now, tell me where he is, and I won't kill you." His eyes track down my body. "For now, at least."

Is every member of his family a disgusting asshole, or what? Can I get a break from them? "I'm afraid I can't help you."

Kai steps out of the apartment, his own gun now held to the stranger. "But I might be able to. Let the girl go, and I won't kill you right here. Don't let her go, and she'll be decorated with your brains, and I assure you, she won't care one bit. Might appreciate it, in fact."

I meet his eyes over the stranger's shoulder, my heart beating erratically in my chest now. Funny how when someone is threatening my life, I feel nothing. Now that Kai is here and can get hurt, I start freaking out. He gives me a little nod, one that says he's here with me, and I can breathe a little deeper for it.

The man spins quickly, moving behind me to grab me around the neck and slide the gun up to my temple. "Kill me, and I kill her. Either way, this ends badly."

Kai must recognize something on the man's face since he slowly lowers his own gun. Not all the way, but enough to give the illusion of backing down. "Calm down, and we can figure out how to help each other get what we want."

Considering I want this man's head in a pickling jar, I doubt we'll all be happy in the end. "Do I get a say in this?"

Kai shakes his head at me, his eyes serious. There's no humor there, not like the last time we faced down a member of Sal's insipid family, which means he knows something I don't. I stay quiet, intent on letting them figure it out, at least until I can come up with some kind of plan that doesn't involve both of us dead.

The man's breath fans my ear as he speaks, and it's enough to make me gag. "I don't want to kill either of you. My instructions are to take you both alive. But she's expendable so…play along, and then we don't have to clean blood out of our clothes today."

Kai takes one step forward, and the gun digs into my head so hard I close my eye on that side to protect it. "What do you want?"

"All I want right now is for you to put your gun on the floor and take one slow step backward. Then we'll all get out of here in one piece."

I sigh. It seems the one somewhat clever of Sal's cousins got to come out and play now. I open my eye again and meet Kai's intent gaze. He looks sad, tired, and like he's given up. It's not a look that agrees with him, and I hate it. He fights me at every turn, never surrendering, and now is the time he stops?

"Are you going to fight me? I will shoot you both and drag you behind me if that's what it takes," he says.

I'm not listening to him because I'm focused on Kai. His sharp cheekbones, the jut of his collarbone. At least he put on pants at some point.

"I'm sorry," he whispers, and I shake my head, telling him I don't want to hear it. Not here, not now. This isn't where we end.

Kai bends and slides the gun across the floor to the other man. I don't even think about it since his focus is on Kai. I scramble to grab the gun out of his grip, the one pressed to my head, but it slips from my fingers as he tips forward and takes the other.

Then all I know is darkness and a sharp pain at the nape of my neck.

## 29

## KAI

When I wake, I know immediately something is wrong. It's dark, blackout dark, and I roll over and retch on the concrete floor. I promised myself I'd never be back here unless I came to burn this place to the ground with the council bitch locked inside.

I slide away from the puke and sit up. Once again, they've taken my clothes, my shoes, everything, and left me in my black boxer briefs. Which means she's planning to do the same things to me she did the last time. The thought is enough to make me want to throw up again.

My vision waves, and I try to clear it, but my head is fuzzy too. They must have dosed me before tossing me in here.

I raise my arm and let it fall to my lap. Yep, definitely sluggish. It feels like the same cocktail they gave me before. There are no noises in the hall, none of the sluggish paths of guards outside my door. Even though it's dark in here, I can't hear anyone else, which means they must be holding Rose elsewhere.

I clench my fists. If they hurt her, then nothing will be able to stop me from destroying this building and every person in it, council member or not.

Carefully, I stand and trace the edge of the bench until it ends, then the wall around to the door. It's locked, of course, but I press my ear to the surface, hoping to at least catch the sound of her voice so I know she's okay.

It's dead silent outside the door, and I curse, sliding down to sit on the cold floor. I hate this fucking place and everything it represents. The last time I was here, that bitch told me she wanted to break me. I told her she'd never be able to do it. Looks like she found the one way in the world she might succeed. If I lose Rose, then I have nothing left.

She doesn't realize that if she breaks me, I'm taking her ass with me. Hopefully, painfully and drenched in her blood.

Those thoughts comfort the blood lust in me, pressing away the darkness and the memories of the last time I stayed in this place. I dread the moment I hear her voice again, but I can't control that. At least for now.

I close my eyes, the grogginess still very present. She's going to need a lot more drugs if she hopes to find me willing. The last time it didn't matter as much. This time, I won't do anything to hurt Rose, and letting this bitch use me would definitely hurt her.

Not that I have much of a choice if she continues to drug me. Even now, I can feel it coursing through my body, slowing me down, pulling at the edges of my concentration. Like this, I'm useless to protect Rose or myself.

I pound my head into the door once, hoping to clear things, but it doesn't help.

There's only one solace to all of this: Rose isn't trapped in this endless dark box with me. Wherever she is being held, I hope it's better. Adrian or maybe my sister's people will come for her soon. Can't have the lost Barone heir resurface only to be lost due to her negligence. Nope, can't have that.

I stand again, wobbling on my feet so hard I hit the door. First, I test the knob again, but no luck. Like last time, I move around the seams of the door, checking the hinges and the floor for any way to break free, but it's as impenetrable as before.

The other side of the room matches its opposite, but I tread carefully, not knowing exactly where I'd been sick earlier. I can smell it in the air, but I'm not willing to get down on the floor and seek it out.

Hopefully, they will clean it up. Thankfully, they did the last time, not leaving me in the stink of sickness for my incarceration. The council bitch wouldn't like that. She wants me clean and unsullied when she uses me for her own pleasure.

The worst part was that I found a little pleasure in it too. Not voluntarily, but between the drugs and the warmth of her body, however much it disgusted me, I had little choice. Sometimes biology wins out.

At those moments, she thought she'd won this great victory, and I was caving to her charms. I can't wait to tell her how much she sickens me.

There's a soft knock on the door, and I turn my head to the sound. Better to hear it. "Hello?" a voice calls. I know her voice almost as well as I know Rose's. It haunts my dreams.

I don't answer her. Instead, I throw myself down on the bench, waiting.

"Hello? I know you're awake in there. I'd like to come in and discuss terms."

I make a noise low in my throat. "By all means, please, come in. I'd be happy to discuss my illegal incarceration and shove your face into the wall a few times."

She laughs, actually laughs, like I'm not dead serious. "Oh, you naughty boy, I do like them with spirit."

I curl my lip and stare toward the sound, waiting to find out what she really wants. She can come in, but that doesn't mean I'll play by her rules.

"I'm opening the door. Now, you behave yourself, or I'll send one of the guards to see Ms. Barone. He likes them on the heftier side and would love to make her acquaintance."

I drop my mouth open. "You kidnap us, and then you have the nerve to insult her? How dare you? I don't want to hear her name in your mouth again."

The door clicks open, and a sliver of light illuminates her thin frame from behind. "Remember what I said."

I clench my fists. "Do you remember what I said? I will kill you. It might not be today, but soon. I warned you what would happen if you came after me."

I try to stare into her eyes, so she knows I'm serious. "Besides, you can do what you want with Rose. She was only my way of gaining protection from the Chicago council. Which seems to be worthless anyway."

She gives me a scathing look. "I didn't take over this city by being an idiot. I know you and Ms. Barone married, and I know you, the consummate rake, wouldn't stoop so low unless you actually had feelings for the girl."

"Do you listen to yourself speak? Rake? Did you just call me a slut in crazy?"

I bring my knees up and hug them to my chest. There's no reason to give her a free show, especially when she's going to take it herself soon anyway.

Her eyes scan my body, the heat there turning my stomach. "Do behave, Kai, or I'll be sure to pay Rose an extra special visit."

I shrug. "As I said, she means nothing to me. You just happen to catch us both together. That doesn't mean we are really together."

"That may be true, but I know Adrian wouldn't take kindly to his new bride's cousin being maimed or killed and left skinned on his doorstep."

That's fair. Adrian's word is law. Anyone in our world knows that. If Rose is hurt in any way, it will be my fault since I'm the one he trusted with her safety and, in the end, Valentina's happiness.

She knows she has me now, her eyes crinkling as she smiles.

"What in the hell do you want from me? I'm not sleeping with you willingly, so there's no reason for you to be here trying to negotiate."

She crosses the room, and I hope she steps in the puke I left there. If there is a god in the universe, he'd make it happen. Sadly, she stops short of that area, her eyes scanning the cell and then landing back on me. "Oh, I think you will cooperate, but as you remember, I don't need you to be willing. I just need you breathing to take what I want."

I want to spit at her, launch myself across the room, and throw her headfirst into a wall. With her delicate frame, she'd break pretty easily. How would she react if the situations were reversed? But I get the desire to want to break someone, to bend to your will. I don't want her broken; I want her fucking destroyed.

"How do you intend to make me cooperate?"

Her eyes call me an idiot while her smile promises pain. "Ms. Barone, of course. I told you I'm not stupid. I promise to keep her safe if you just come to my bed willingly."

"The only reason she was in danger in the first place was because of your vendetta against me."

She clasps her hands in front of her silk robe. "Well then, I guess you shouldn't have dragged her into this by aligning yourself with her."

It hits me...she's fucking jealous.

Somehow, she found out I'd gone off alone with Rose to hide, and she got jealous. It's the only thing that makes sense. The only thing that explains why she'd come after me so hard after she agreed with Adrian not to pursue me until after the hearing. I keep that little nugget to myself for the moment and try to think of how to use it to my advantage.

If I can get within a foot of her, I can snap her neck as easily as a twig. It was a lot harder when she tied you to a bed and rode you like her own personal saddle horse.

I uncurl from the stool, and she takes a step back, her guards hovering at the door. When I get closer, she wards me off with one hand. "Stop, or I will have them taser you. It would be unfortunate since I'd do the same to dear Rose for the trouble of forcing me to wait."

I give her a seductive look. A mask I'd perfected from being society's pretty playboy. It has brought many a woman and man to their knees. And they always spill their secrets. It's usually a matter of whether they took my cock into their mouths before or after. "You want me, I know you do. I won't submit willingly, not in a million years, but maybe, you can win me over in time."

"How?" she breathes. I take one more experimental step forward, about to reach for her, when the guards are suddenly there, dragging me back.

I fight them and stare her down. "I guess you'll never find out now."

She pulls a syringe from her robe pocket. "Submit, come willingly, and I'll make sure Rose doesn't end up mutilated in a dumpster."

Fuck. She wants to do it. Killing Rose would be a power trip for her. With one shot, she'd eliminate her competition for me and also a competitor for power once Rose comes into her own as a Barone. She wants nothing more than for me to give her an excuse. I'm good at reading people, and she is counting the seconds.

I shake the guards off, and she waves them away. Then with a sneer meant only for her, I hold out my arm to take the syringe. She passes it to the guard to administer, and in a minute, I feel its effects merge with whatever is already in my system. The world is swimming in and out of focus when I feel hands on me.

I lash out until my body grows loose and languid, not allowing me to do much more than stumble along the hallway they drag me down. In the room, I smell the cloying disgusting scent of the council bitch's perfume. It's a smell that lingers and haunts me.

I cough, choking on it, as they tie me to the bed. So I guess this will be just like last time. Only, this time, she has one big-ass bargaining chip to keep me compliant.

If she succeeds, and I don't see how she won't, I hope Adrian puts me out of my misery when it's over. There's no coming back this time.

## 30

## ROSE

*I* wake with a blistering headache in a dark room that smells of dust and bleach. That can't be a good sign. The bed is hard, and the bedding material is scratchy and rustles as I carefully sit up. Where the hell am I?

Definitely not in the Chicago penthouse, nor do I think I am in Adrian and Valentina's home? Adrian wouldn't need to abduct us to get us to come with him.

My money is on the council bitch who is obsessed with Kai. A part of me is happy I might learn the story there, but I'm also dreading it. If it was something that shook Kai, of all people, it can't be a good thing. A woebegone ex looking to make amends or something. If only.

I carefully ease off the bed to stand. I'm not as wobbly as I was before, but my feet are bare. At least I'm still wearing the same jeans and T-shirt I'd put on before Kai's and my argument.

Is this my fault? Did my call to Valentina set this in motion? Maybe they bugged the phone lines to pinpoint where we were located. That seems pretty low-tech, but I can't think of another reason Kai would be so angry with me for making a call, nor that these goons grabbed us such a short time later.

My head pounds, and this is not the time to try to rationalize this mess. Not when every step makes me want to pitch forward and puke.

I rub my temples and survey the door. It's probably locked, but it never hurts to try in a situation like this. With a long inhale, I reach out and turn the doorknob. It opens easily since apparently someone left it unlocked. Maybe luck is on my side today.

I step into the dark hallway and check both ends. Nothing.

There isn't one of those you are here in the underground lair maps on the wall, so I pick a direction and jog the long length of the hall.

The corner bends to the left, and I run straight into a hulking guard, complete with night baton and gun strapped to his side. Perfect. Fate can go fuck itself.

He snatches me by the arm and drags me alongside him. "Perfect timing. The mistress wants a word with you."

"The mistress? Are we in some kind of kink den?"

He frowns down at me like I'm an idiot and walks faster so I am almost stumbling to keep up. All the while, my feet are freezing on the painted concrete floors. If they are going to kidnap people, they could at least get a nice runner.

When we stop outside a door, I eye his holster and very carefully unclip the side of it. When he doesn't call me out immediately, I sigh, relieved. If I manage to get his gun, great. If not, maybe someone else can grab it and save us from this *SAW* wannabe hellhole.

He shoves me through the door first, and I glance around, immediately hunting for a weapon. At least until I see the bed, covered in black silk bedding, with Kai tied up at the four posters. His tan skin looks pale against all that black, and as I move closer, I see he's naked. Naked and completely hard.

I rush to the bedside and try to get the knots loose, but they are tight, and it's useless. There aren't any weapons I can see, and I don't have anything on me. I face the guard. "Let him go. What are you doing to him?"

His lip curls up in disgust. "Not me who's fucking him. He's for the mistress."

The fuck he is. Anger steamrolls my fear, and I glare as I return to the bedside to see if I can wake him up. Nothing. Not even a gentle slap to the face is enough to bring him around. "What the hell is going on here?"

I obviously missed something, and I'm scared that if I find out too late, then I won't be able to save either of us. The guard isn't giving me anything. The room looks sparse, but what furniture there is seems to be high-end. Stuff like Valentina's dad would buy to impress people who came to the house.

I face the guard again. "Let him go. Please. I'll stay, and you can have me instead."

This earns me another pitying glance. "As I said, he's not for me. He's for the mistress."

The sound of my name keeps me from punching the guard and likely getting smashed to bits by his big meaty hands. I race back to Kai's bedside and brush my thumb along his cheek. "Hi, you're alive. I'm so relieved."

"You're beautiful."

I blink. "Well, thank you, but not necessarily something that matters at the moment."

He lifts his head to look at me, but it wobbles back like a bobblehead until he gives up. "No, you're beautiful. You don't understand. I love you."

His words pierce me, not because he said he loves me, but because he said it now while he's drugged and unsure if he's going to survive. It's a deathbed confession, not a declaration of his feelings. I hop up to press my forehead against his. "I love you too, you big idiot. Now we need to figure out how to get you out of here."

"Kiss me," he murmurs.

I give him a soft peck, and he scoffs at me. Drugged out of his mind, and he still scoffs for not giving him a good enough kiss. "See if I kiss you later when we get out of this mess."

A soft voice behind me says, "Oh, I don't believe you'll need to worry about that."

I turn and wish I hadn't. An older woman, maybe mid-fifties, is standing there in black high heels and a silk robe covering her very thin-looking assets. "Uh...who are you?"

She waves at me, the same imperious wave Kai's sister uses.

It hits me. "You must be the council bitch."

As she moves around the bed to the opposite side, she gives me a dirty little glare. "Is that what he calls me?"

I snort. "Amongst other things. What are we doing here?"

Her gaze shifts to Kai and his spread body on the bed. I want to jab her eyes out for the way she's looking at him.

"He's here for me. You are here for, I don't know what, power maneuvers…" She leans into him and shakes his shoulder. When he wakes and finally sees her, he recoils, jamming his head against his opposite arm. "Stop pretending you didn't agree to this. As agreed, your friend is safe and sound. Now, it's time for you to fulfill your side of the bargain."

"No," he whispers, and I recognize the panicked look in his eyes. He didn't agree to this, and he'd never agree. Even if it meant keeping me safe. If he did agree under those conditions, I'm going to kill him myself because I'd rather be dead than force him to endure whatever is about to happen.

"What's going on here? I demand you release us both. We are under the protection of the Chicago council."

"Yes," she mocks. "But no one told you that sanctuary is tenuous when the season is open. Currently, the leaders there are fair game. They don't give a shit about you and the head councilwoman's brother. They are fighting for their seats and their lives right now."

I should be concerned and try to find a way to warn Kai's sister, but I wasn't lying when I told this lady I don't care about her. Right now, the only person I care about is Kai, and wrenching this woman's head from her neck.

Wait. Her words sink in, as does her conversation with Kai. "What did you do?" I'm not sure if I'm addressing Kai or her.

"Why, he traded himself for your life, my dear. Now that I have him under my control, I plan to make sure you can't get in the way, so don't get too excited."

I want to smack him again, harder this time. "What the hell?"

He stirs, trying to look at me again, but I turn away, giving him my back while I try to figure out how we can take care of this problem. When I spin again, I face the councilwoman. "Any chance you're interested in women?"

She sneers. "No, not a chance in hell." She says it like I'm coming on to her for my own benefit. Gross.

"Well, then how do we fix this?"

She keeps her eyes on Kai as she answers. "Considering the trouble I went through to acquire him, nothing will entice me to give him up."

I never thought I'd meet someone as disgusting as Sal and his family. Another person who buys and sells humans for their own needs, never caring what happens after they take what they want.

I want to yell at her, at Kai, force them to end this stupid agreement and see reason. But I can tell by the heat in her eyes when she looks at him that it won't happen. She wants him in the same way I do. And that sort of need isn't tame, isn't reasoned with, isn't something I can force her to ignore.

If she keeps touching him, though, I might try to kill her.

The guard shifts closer to me as if he can sense my resentment, the fury rising in my blood. "You can't do this," I try one more time.

She still doesn't bother to look at me. Instead, she runs her nails up Kai's shin. "I can do whatever I want. That's what makes us different, Ms. Barone. You may have been born in this world, but you'll never be a part of it."

I take a step forward, about to yank her off the bed by her cheaply dyed hair. Of course, the guard gets to me first, wrapping an arm around my waist to hold me back. I stop struggling and glare up at him. "Any chance you can let me go, and then we pretend none of this ever happened. After I kill her, of course."

He blinks as if I've surprised him. "No, no, we can't. Besides, you couldn't afford me."

Somehow that statement sounds vaguely sexual. What the fuck is in the water around here?

## 31

## KAI

I try to lift myself, bending, moving, sliding, anything to get off this bed and get to her. To remove that filthy guard's hands from her skin. "Let her go!" I yell, but it comes out garbled and slurred.

Even with her under their control, I'm relieved she's alive, safe, and looks unharmed, outside of the seriously pissed-off look in her eyes. If she finds out I did this to protect her, then she might not forgive me for it. But she'll be alive, and in the end, when it's all over, I'll be dead regardless. At least if Adrian is the friend, I know him to be.

She can hate me and live.

But I'll love her until the second I'm dead. Maybe even after.

I try to say her name, but all that comes out of my mouth is drool. I glare at the bitch near the end of the bed, and I want to scream. Is this sexy? Is this the kind of man she wants? I can't even function properly.

Rose pleads with her and the guard to let us go, but that's never going to happen. She's wasting her breath.

"Rose," I manage.

Her eyes lock to mine, and she struggles harder. "Don't you dare give up, you bastard. You refused to let me do it, and I sure as hell won't allow you to. Consider it payback for all the times you pushed me."

I deserve that and her anger. If I'd been more vigilant and less distracted, then neither of us would have been taken.

The council bitch climbs up beside me on the bed, so close I can feel the knobby bones of her knees. I struggle against the bonds. "No, don't. Not in front of Rose."

She narrows her eyes and shakes her head, placing a hand on my abs. "Oh no, the time for negotiation has passed. She should watch, learn who your new master is."

Fucking hell, she's really going to do this, right in front of the guard, in front of Rose. The only reason I can think of is to punish us both.

Despite my disgust of the woman, my dick is hard. I ignore it, but she doesn't, her eyes sliding there covetously. She must have put some kind of Viagra or something in her little drug cocktail, just like she had to do last time.

I mumble a second and then get hold of the words in my foggy brain. "It must gall you to know you can't get me hard on your own. That you have to drug me into it." I flick my chin toward Rose. "She can do it just by looking at me. Just by breathing too closely to me. You'll only ever get me by force and by pharmaceutical application."

She slaps me hard, but I only smile. "You can't hit worth a damn either."

For a second, she leans away and produces a knife. "I might not have the strength you do, but this will do just fine if you want to play games."

She trails the tip of the knife down my belly to rest gently against the head of my cock. "If I can't have you, no one will. Don't make me unman you before I even get to have a ride."

Bile rises in my throat, and I can't hold my head up anymore. She takes it as my submission and pulls the blade away. It disappears under the bed again, and she resettles near my hip. When she throws one thigh over top of my pelvis, I struggle harder. She can fucking stab me for all I care. I'm not going to make it easier for her to rape me.

I buck my hips upward, and for a second, she thinks she's won, that I'm finally trying to meet her, but I get my knee sideways enough that I hit her in the rib cage hard enough to knock her off my body.

She lets out a satisfying *oomph* and then scrambles farther away. From somewhere nearby, Rose laughs. "He's a bastard, but he's going to make you work for it, isn't he?"

"Shut the hell up," the council bitch snaps. "I didn't ask your opinion, and if you keep talking, I'll be sure to get the gag. Or maybe I'll bring you closer, put your face on the bed while I fuck him, let you see how much he loves to give me his cock."

There's the sound of a scuffle, and Rose screaming obscenities, then silence. The woman is doing this to punish me now, making me cooperate, and it might just damn work.

The door opens and closes, and Rose says my name softly. "Get up. You have to try to get out of those ropes while she's gone."

The guard speaks up. "What the hell do you think I'm here for?"

I lift my head in time to watch her glare at him while he holds her arms behind her back. "You're here to raise my body count when I get free again."

He doesn't look convinced, but her retort makes me smile. That's my fucking girl.

The woman returns a minute later, and I've lost all the energy to fight. I can't even move my arms anymore. My legs are tightened down, then my wrists. So tight it's cutting off circulation and leaving my fingertips to tingle.

She produces another syringe and holds it up to the light to measure the contents of her little cocktail. "I told you not to play games with me, but you can't just give in, can you?"

I snort, my mouth thick, my tongue heavy. But I can see her, and I hope she sees the contempt in my eyes, the disgust, and how much I want to rip her limb from limb.

She brings the syringe near my arm, and Rose screams at her. "Stop this, please, don't give him anymore. Can't you see you'll kill him if you do? He's already out of it enough. I thought you wanted to fuck a man, not a corpse."

The council bitch steps back toward Rose. "You have no idea what I want, little girl, nor can you fully comprehend what kind of man he is or what he can do for me. You know nothing about our relationship."

I sneer at the word as if I'd ever get within ten feet of her. Once upon a time, I'd been that man, easily swayed by a pretty smile or a handsome face, but not anymore. And she wouldn't have tempted me anyway. Not with the cruelty written into every line of her face.

Rose shouts again, and I look up to realize I've missed something. The guard is holding his face, and somehow Rose has gotten his gun.

Well, this took a turn. I'm smiling like an idiot, but I don't even care. Not when she looks so strong, so fierce, trying to protect us.

"Rose," I whisper, but only a moan comes out.

Her voice reaches me again. "Give me that shit." She snatches the syringe and throws it away.

I can't keep my head up much longer, but I have to watch her, to look at her, to make sure she stays safe, and now free.

The ropes are too tight, and my limbs too heavy to break out, though. I can't do anything but watch as Rose faces them down with the guard's gun. I pray she remembers what I taught her about firing it.

Rose points the gun at the council bitch and motions for her to back away from me. When the cloying scent of her perfume recedes, I relax into the bed a little bit more, no longer tense, waiting for her to touch me again.

"Touch him again, and I'll kill you," Rose says, a conviction in her voice that would make me hard if I wasn't already. This is different, though. It stirs my soul as well as my body.

Rose moves beside me so I can see her face without straining my neck. "Hi," I whisper.

"Hi," she says, and I close my eyes, savoring the sight of her above me. Maybe it will be okay this time.

## 32

## ROSE

*I* understand now. The fear I've seen in his eyes, the way he holds me, pushes me, makes me stronger even when it's uncomfortable. I get it.

Seeing him on that bed, strapped down naked, breaks my heart. This was me not too long ago, and I won't let him stay that way, not even if it means sacrificing myself to save him.

He lifts his head when I rush to his side, trying to figure out the rope so I can get him loose. There's shame on his face as he looks away, so I can't see more of it. I know that shame too. Every second he is here breaks something in me, and I can't bring him back the same way he's saved me. I'm not strong enough.

I grapple with the ropes and then lean over the side of the bed. "Kai, look at me."

But he's groggy, his eyes going hazy. I have no idea what kind of drugs she's given him. I hate this woman so much.

I spin to look around the room and lock eyes with the bitch. "What did you give him? How do I bring him out of this?"

She shrugs, seemingly completely unconcerned by the fact that I'm pointing a gun at her. My only conclusion is she thinks I won't shoot her.

I turn to face the guard, give him a smile, and shoot him in the head. He hits the floor with a loud thud, and I face the woman again. "Now, let's have a real conversation."

She inclines her head, finally a bit of wariness in her gaze. "By all means, what do you want to talk about?"

I face Kai and hope he can hear me. "Kai, wake up for me. I'm going to get you out of here. Just hang on for a second while I deal with this."

The council bitch, with her spider thin body in her black silk robe, still seems a little too unconcerned about me. I don't like it because if she is indifferent, she's unlikely to negotiate for what I want.

"What did you give him?"

With a sigh, she shrugs again. "Maybe a little Viagra to make sure he has the stamina I need to get what I want from him."

I want to press the gun into her mouth and watch her brains explode out of the back of her head right now. It's unreal how vibrant the fantasy of it is in my mind. I didn't get to kill Sal, but I sure as hell can kill this woman who hurt Kai. And I don't think I'd feel a single bit of remorse for it.

The guard, maybe, since he was just doing his job. But this bitch? No. I've got no fucks, and I'm not even going to try to find any.

"You are a piece of shit. I hope you know that. You couldn't go out and find a willing man? You have to take what you can't have."

She stares at me, bored, which only makes me angrier.

I point toward Kai. "What do you even want with him? He's the second in command to your enemy, and he's a dick about half of the time."

Now her red mouth turns up in an unhinged smile. "Well, the other half of the time is worth the attitude, and if I really don't like them, I just keep them drugged until they are of no use to me."

"You mean if they can't get it up anymore, right?"

"Your words, not mine. I was trying to be kind."

I shake my head, licking my lips, giving myself touchstones so I don't pistol whip this bitch in her too-thin face. "You are disgusting. Trash. I hope you know that."

"That would be your opinion, young lady, but I'd watch how you speak to your councilwoman. You are, after all, still under my jurisdiction, Rose Barone."

It's chilling that she knows my name when Kai didn't even know it before. "What did you plan to do with him? Keep him locked here or use him and kill him?"

She turns her attention to Kai, creeping closer to him. I nudge her shoulder with the muzzle of the gun. "Nope, not in this lifetime. Back away."

"To answer your question, I planned to just play with him a little bit. It's so much fun to break the ones who think they are the strongest, and trust me, dear, they all break."

I don't need to trust her. I've seen it, felt it, and I wouldn't allow her to do that to another person ever again. She just hasn't figured it out yet.

She shifts a little bit, and I realize too late she's within touching distance of him. When she lifts her hand, I raise mine, pointing the gun at her face again. "Don't even think about it."

"He was my little play toy before he became yours." She wraps her bony hand around his calf, so I point the gun and shoot her in the leg. For someone so thin, she goes down like a sack of rocks, hitting the floor almost as loudly as the bigger guard.

"I did tell you not to touch him."

She glares up at me, her hand clamped on her leg. It's interesting that she seems unfazed otherwise. "You are just a whore for rent, disposable. I'm the real deal," she says, her tone dripping ice. "You can do what you want to me, but you'll be caught, you'll be punished, and he will join you."

I shrug. "And your little dog too."

This makes her curl her lip at me. Oh, someone is touchy about her age then. Good to know.

"You can stand if you're able, but if you put one more finger on him, I will kill you. Now, was it just you who used him, or did you call your friends and let them have a turn too?"

For a second, she seems confused before she clears her features to indifference again. "I'm not sure what you are implying."

"All psychos are the same. Some of you like to share your...toys. I just wanted to make sure I didn't have another list of people to go hunt down after you."

I stare down at the piece of human filth I am excited to end. She glares back at me and then lunges over the end of the bed to try to reach the gun. A few more feet and she might have made it, well, if I hadn't already shot her.

"Nice try, but I'm younger and faster, and I really want to kill you, so don't push it and end this too prematurely."

She spits on the floor between us, and I shake my head. "Classy, super classy. Tell me again how you are so much better than me."

"You will never be one of us, even if you do manage to trap him into a relationship with you, and that's a big if considering your...girth, you will never be a part of this society."

I chuckle and run my hand over the slight belly I've gained from eating more regularly again. "Well, when he's on his knees eating me out, he doesn't seem to mind something soft to rest his head against. At least, that's how I see it."

"What about you? Does he have a problem with your hip bones threatening to stab him?"

She stiffens, and I wave at her. "You're the one who went there first. I was happy to continue trading angry barbs, but you had to make it personal."

It's already personal, with Kai strapped to that bed, but god, I hate this woman, and toying with her makes me feel just a little bit better.

Carefully, she uses the bed to stand, keeping her weight off her injured leg. I note she is equally careful not to touch Kai in her use of the bed. "Maybe we have more in common than I thought. Perhaps we can discuss this."

"You can discuss this. I can stand here and mock you until you figure out there's nothing you can give me that I want."

"Perhaps a trade? I give you a place here, amongst us, a house, money. All you have to do is leave him here. Give him to me, and you can have anything you want."

I gag at the thought of leaving him in this place, not for anything, and it hurts my heart that she might have made a deal like this before, which is why she's attempting to do it now. "Wow, you have no idea how to read a person, do you? I don't want to be a part of your society. I doubt most people in said society want to be a part of it, especially if you're the leader. No wonder things are so fucked up around here."

She sniffs, raising her chin. "I take exception to that statement; things are perfectly fine."

I narrow my eyes and tilt my head to Kai. "If things were perfectly fine, you wouldn't have to kidnap your sex partners and drug them, now would you? You disgust me. All of your kind disgusts me."

This time, she smiles, cruel and cold. "He is one of our kind, little girl, born and bred."

"Well, that's not something he can help, and he's right on the front line trying to fix what he had a hand in breaking. You simply revel in the chaos."

"Chaos does pay the bills."

I wave the gun between us. "We aren't the same. I may have been born in this fucked-up world, but I'm nothing like you. Proudly so."

"And him? What will you do with him when he wants to go back to Chicago, join his sister, and become part of that little organization with just as many morally inept people?"

"I don't give a fuck about his crazy-ass sister."

She shrugs, a little too calm now. "Just as well. I did hear the season is open."

I might not have any idea what she's saying, but I know the tone of a threat when I hear one. "You think she doesn't have her own protection out there. I'm sure she can take care of herself."

"But she didn't do a single thing to protect you, right? Not when you needed it most. Maybe she thinks her brother will inherit the Barone dynasty when you're gone. A clever ploy to get her greedy little hands on your family money."

I laugh. "I don't have any money. If my family did, I sure as hell don't know where it is right now."

"Then let me give you money. Set you up here."

"In exchange for Kai, right? That's the deal. Would you even let me walk out of here after I shot you?"

Another cold, cruel smile. "Try it and find out."

I match her little grin and shake my head. "No, I don't need to. What you should know is I never intended to let you walk out of here alive. Not for one second, not for all the money in the world."

"Everyone wants something."

I step up to the bed and run my hand up Kai's still arm. "Yes, everyone wants something. And right now, I want my husband's rapist to die violently, painfully."

Her eyes go wide a second before I pull the trigger. I walk around the side of the bed to kneel next to her. Blood is pouring from the wound in her chest, but she's still alive. Alive enough to hear me at least.

"That man is my husband. He belongs to me. You will never touch him again."

I shouldn't take pleasure in watching someone's life leave their eyes. Hell, from my experiences, I should be running the other way. Yet as the councilwoman dies, her blood staining my bare feet, I'm strangely okay with this.

## 33

# KAI

The guard crumples to the floor, the woman soon after, and I feel sad for Rose, that she had to do that to save me. The last time she held a gun in her hand, she couldn't pull the trigger, but this time, she didn't hesitate.

She comes around the bed, still in the same clothes from earlier, and something loosens in my chest since I'd been worrying someone might have hurt her, put her through the same things I'd endured.

She is so beautiful, splattered in the councilwoman's blood. So strong, and my heart aches just to look at her.

"Come here, come over here so I can touch you."

She huffs out a laugh. "You, sir, are drugged up. Relax, and let me get you out of this." Her fingers dig into the knots, but she can't loosen them. "What the hell? Was this woman in the Navy or something? Shit."

It doesn't matter. I can't wait any longer. "Get up here, please. I need you."

She stills, staring at me, then really looking down the length of my body where my cock is hard and bouncing against my abs with every twitch. "Oh, you mean...?"

"Now, get up here and ride my dick, now."

I think she's going to protest, and she keeps grumbling as she climbs onto the bed, saturated with the woman's blood. She is splattered, but I'm covered in it since I'd been behind her when Rose had pulled the trigger.

She has to wiggle out of her pants and frowns as they get covered in red. "What do you...? Are you sure about this? You've been drugged. You might not really want me to touch you right now."

I jerk at the ropes, trying to get to her. "Please, Rose, don't make me suffer. Come here and ride me. I need to feel you around me."

She swallows hard and then crawls up my body, slipping in the blood until she's almost as covered as I am. "Do it," I urge when her core slides up my length. "Do it. Do it. Do it. Please, don't make me beg."

"I'm not going to make you beg. Calm the hell down. I'm just not sure how I feel about fucking you covered in someone's blood is all."

"Then get closer, and I'll make sure you're good and ready for me."

With another heavy frown, she situates herself against my cock and then lifts it. I jolt at her soft fingers, the slick blood coating me, the way the heat of her body is like nothing else. "This is so unsanitary," she groans. But she closes her eyes as she carefully slides down my length.

In the back of my mind, I know some kind of Viagra had to be mixed into the woman's drug cocktail, but I don't care. All I can think about is Rose riding me. Rose taking her pleasure. Rose leaving nothing left after she's done.

"How does that feel?" I lock my eyes on her. "Do you like the way my cock stretches you wide, how you fit against me so perfectly?"

She swallows hard and nods. "Yes, it feels good."

"Faster," I command. "Faster. I want to hear our bodies slapping together. I want you to shift forward so my cock rubs against your clit."

Another huff, but she does as I direct, her hands splayed on my belly for balance while she rocks back onto me. Fuck, she feels so good, so tight and warm. I'm not going to last much longer, and even so, I already know it's not going to be enough. I already want more of her, and neither of us has even come yet.

"I want my hands, Rose. I need to touch you. Let me loose."

She jerks to a halt, her heavy breathing erratic. "Your hands." She scans the bed, the floor, and then spots something over the other side. She bends down, almost enough to be painful for me, but sits back up with a knife clutched tight in her grasp. "This will work."

She quickly saws through the bindings, and the second I'm free, I sit up and wrap my arms around her. "There we go. This is how it's supposed to be. I'm meant to touch you, taste you, through this."

"Um...I think you're still drugged."

I duck my head and clamp my lips around her nipple through her shirt and her bra. "I'm a little groggy, but that's it. I just don't want to keep my hands off you."

She cups my cheeks, turning my face up again to look into my eyes. "Then don't. Now, this is your party. So fuck me, and make it good."

I smile, drag her into me from the small of her back, and wrap my legs underneath her. "Are you ready?"

She nods once and holds my shoulders. I use my abs, my thighs, my hips, everything to pound into her from below, and when my cock drags over her sensitive clit, I keep a steady rhythm there. "Are you going to come on my cock like a good little girl?"

Her nod is her only answer as she's biting her bottom lip to keep from screaming.

When she starts to clamp around me, a whimpering sound escapes her, then a mumbled, "I'm coming. I'm coming."

I don't hold myself back anymore. It takes a moment to get there, but the wet hot glide of her, and the rhythmic pulse of her own orgasm is enough to shove me over the cliff. I press my forehead into her shoulder as I ride out the wave of pleasure, letting it fizzle slowly, coming back to myself.

I'm still a bit hazy, and now my legs feel like rubber, but overall, I wasn't hurt. That's good. The last time, she spared me nothing. I suppose the councilwoman didn't have me long enough this time.

"Hey," Rose whispers against my mouth. "I'm right here. It's me you're with. Stay with me. Right here."

I nod, dragging the clean scent of her into my lungs. "My Rose." She's so perfect.

The door opens a second later, and I'm so groggy that the man walks into the room before I can react and wrap myself around Rose. "Who are you?"

He studies the scene, coming in and out of focus for me. "Well, this looks positively barbaric."

Something about him seems familiar. He's tall, as tall as Adrian. His suit rivals one of my own, and the perfectly styled dark curls on his head lead me to only one answer. "You're council."

He nods and crouches to look at the council woman's chest. "Did you do this?"

Rose opens her mouth, but I shake my head. "Yes, I did it."

He wipes his hands on her silk robe and stands to face us again, his hands tucked into his pockets. I'm forgetting something with the drugs and the sex clouding my brain. It hits me a second later. He's the councilman Andrea took for ransom when we saved Adrian.

"Who are you?"

He moves to the bodyguard. "Don't worry about that right now. The only thing you need to worry about is getting out of here."

As if on cue, Adrian and Michail burst into the room, coming up short behind the immaculate councilman. He waves toward the bed, and Adrian moves first. Rose's face goes even more red to match the blood dotting her skin as she slides off me and dives for her pants. "No one look at her, not one fucking person look at her."

Adrian grabs me under the arms. "You're the naked one, Kai. No one is going to be looking at her, trust me."

I'm covered in blood, but it's smeared like someone has fingerpainted my skin with it, and in a way, I guess she has. It feels like a claiming, and I don't hate it, especially not as I step over the councilwoman's corpse to reach the door.

We pause at the entry, Adrian studying the council member. "What do you want?"

His focus is on the bodies again. "Nothing you can give me. I'll take care of this. Get your friend out of here. I can't say many will be sad to see her gone."

I can agree with that. Rose rushes forward to Michail's side, then through the door first. A second later, we are following, Adrian still scowling, no doubt trying to figure out what the councilman wants and why he's helping us to begin with. All good questions, but none my drug-addled mind can deal with at the moment.

I sink into my friend's hold and let myself be carried out of those dark dungeons and then gently laid in the back of an SUV. Rose settles my head on her soft thigh, stroking my cheek. "You're safe," she says again.

I clutch her hand, trying to tell her all the things crowding my mind right now. So many words I can't say, not with so many people watching us.

Rose squeezes my hand back and addresses my friends. "What will happen now? Will they send me back to that place for killing her?"

I open my mouth to explain the rules, but nothing comes out. Adrian answers in my silence. "No, the season is currently open, so what you did is, by our laws, perfectly acceptable. Even more so when the news spreads about how it happened. But we'll have to keep a close eye on you. Rather, Kai will have to. Others will see you as a threat and seek to get rid of you before you can get rid of them."

This makes her laugh. "The only threats I intend to neutralize are the ones who come for me and mine."

Pressure sits on my chest at her words. She fits right in with our family; she just has no idea yet since she doesn't know them. We'd all do anything for each other.

Michail meets my eyes in the mirror, nodding his approval. He doesn't need to know she was mine from the moment I carried her out of Novak's house and deposited her into the doctor's waiting arms. She opened her eyes then and whispered Valentina's name. Even dying, she wanted to save her cousin, her sister, from suffering.

Looks like fate intervened several times in her life, for both good and bad.

We ride the rest of the trip in silence, then take the helicopter to the penthouse. It's a tiring trip for anyone, but I'm barely stumbling along, the pants they gave me low on my hips, already stained with the dried blood on my skin.

When I can open my eyes again, I seek out Rose to make sure she's still here. She gives me her hand, refusing to let me go unless necessary. Knowing she's here makes the whole thing easier since I know she'll be with me when I wake up.

The penthouse looks the same, and I'm so happy to be home I can't even say the words. Which is fine since no one needs to hear them.

Valentina comes from somewhere and surveys all of us. "Oh, my god, is that all your blood?"

I can't tell her Rose killed the councilwoman since it's not my story to tell. "None of it, actually. I'll be fine, promise."

She sags in relief, her eyes searching out her cousin, who has already followed Adrian, no doubt pestering him for a doctor.

I sink to my knees on the hardwood and close my eyes.

Michail pats me on the back. "Come on, buddy, let's get you in bed so the doc can have a look. You can't stay here on the cold floor, or someone will murder me for allowing it."

When I don't respond, he shifts around me to get my arm over his shoulder and heave me to my feet. I'm home, so it doesn't matter where I lay my head now.

## 34

## ROSE

*I* am torn between keeping my eyes on my husband and following the clean lines and high-end decorations of Adrian's penthouse—or more like a compound, by its look. I can't complain, though, since it means he is keeping Valentina safe. I spot the view as we step off the elevator, and I want to go check it out, but Kai comes first.

Adrian and Michail haul Kai between them to his suite, and I trail the men, fussing over how gently they lay him on the dove gray coverlet.

I wave at Kai, staring down Adrian. "Can we get a doctor in here, now?"

He narrows his eyes at me, his frown shifting to a scowl, one I give right back. For some reason, he must be mistaking me for a simpering fool if he thinks I won't demand Kai be cared for. It's the reason we came here after all, and not to his own family.

Adrian sends a text on his phone and then sits on the bed next to Kai. I'm two seconds from fussing about it when Kai reaches out to take my hand.

"You might not approve, but we're married, official, legally," Kai tells him, caressing my fingers.

Adrian pulls something out of his breast pocket. "I heard rumors you took a wife, although they reported it was a marriage of convenience."

I nudge Kai with my shoulder. "There is nothing at all convenient about this man."

His piercing eyes focus on me, and I can see how Val became ensnared. He seems to be able to see you from the inside out. It's mesmerizing and creepy to me.

The doctor rushes into the room, saving me from having to make small talk with him, though.

We move off the bed and take up similar stances at the end of the bed to monitor the doctor's progress.

The doctor checks his vitals and looks at Adrian over his shoulder. "Do you know what drugs he was given?"

Adrian crosses his arms and scowls; she doesn't need to look at him to know what he's thinking. One of them should have grabbed the drugs so the doctor could treat him effectively. An idiot move on all our parts. To be fair, we'd been focused on the dead councilwoman and then the new council member catching us red-handed.

Michail lingers near the door, keeping a sharp eye on both Kai and Adrian. I wonder if I fall under his supervision now too.

When the doctor finishes, he prods the back of Kai's head where he'd been knocked out. Nothing seems to be wrong, but the doctor warns me to wake him up every so often and make sure he drinks lots of water on top of the IV.

I wait, barely constrained, until the doctor sets up an IV and leaves Kai to Adrian and me again.

"If you have something better to do, I can take care of him," I say, not taking my gaze from Kai's now that I have him again.

Adrian lingers at the end of the bed, watching Kai, watching us, but it doesn't bother me. He's worried about his friend, and I can understand that. I snuggle up under Kai's arm, and he shifts me into him so my legs are entwined along his longer ones.

Finally, Adrian nods to Kai and walks out without another word.

"Is he always like that?"

Kai laughs. "Yes, he is, except when he's around Valentina. She brings out a different side of him. Just like you do for me."

I smile and let him tighten his grip to squeeze me. "Oh, you want to see what's in the box?"

I eye the tiny square he sets flat on the middle of his chest. "Some kind of jewelry, I assume."

He opens the box, and my eyes shoot straight to the giant diamond in the middle. "Holy shit, you'd need your own security team to wear that outside."

Gently, he slides the band onto my finger. Of course, it fits perfectly. "How did he know?"

Kai lays me back down and holds my hand up so we can both admire the sparkle of the diamond. "He's good at those kinds of things, the smaller details."

I drop my hand and roll to rest my cheek on his upper chest. "You didn't have to give me a ring."

"You think Valentina would feel the same way once she hears we are married and how we had to do it? I'm hoping the giant diamond will show her how much I really do care."

I swat at his chest and roll my eyes. A voice breaks in from the doorway. "If you want to show me you care about my cousin, Kai, you could have invited me to the wedding."

Gently, I climb off the bed and gather my cousin, my sister, into my arms. We both squeeze each other until we can't stand it any longer and stare into each other's faces.

"You've lost weight," she mentions.

"You're pregnant?" I don't hide the shock in my tone, staring between Kai and Val.

He huffs. "I told you a while ago. You don't remember?"

I frame my hands around her slight baby bump. "Well, there's a difference between informing and seeing the actual proof with my own eyes."

She tips her head toward me. "What about you, are you guys being safe?"

I don't mention how I rode him covered in the evil queen's blood, and neither of us used protection. If it happens, it happens, and I don't think I'll be upset about it. "Yes, we are being safe. Not a topic I want to go into, though, if that's okay with you."

She shrugs, and then leaves me to kiss Kai on the cheek. "We've missed you around here."

"You mean Adrian has missed me, and he's driving you insane with his hovering?"

Her smile makes my stomach flutter, reminding me of our childhood when smiles weren't so precious and rare as they became when we got older.

Val heads for the door, and Kai tilts his head after her. "You can go with her, catch up, spend time together."

I climb onto the bed and curl up beside him again. "Nope, I need to stay here and protect you from cougars on power trips."

He chuckles, and I wince. "Sorry, too soon?"

"No, I've already forgotten about her."

I kiss him softly, but he doesn't let me get off easy, cupping the back of my head, holding me against him until I see stars and am breathing so fast I have to calm my heart again.

"You're supposed to be resting. If Adrian finds out, he'll be mad at me, and I fear what his version of a punishment will be."

"Yeah, it might not be your thing." Kai kisses my forehead, and I settle against him once more.

"Are we going to get pregnant? We weren't exactly safe back there. What do you think about it?"

He shrugs. "If she's your baby, then I'll love her no matter what."

"She'll be your baby too, so…you'll have to live with both of our chaos demons living in one child. That doesn't sound terrifying?"

Another shrug. "No, challenging, of course, but not scary."

I shake my head, pinching my ear between us. "You're not the one who has to shoot a watermelon out of there, so *you* wouldn't have anything to fear."

He tries to pull me over onto his lap, but I resist. "You need to rest, remember? I'm not having sex with you right now."

His eyes twinkle in the setting sun beyond the windows, but I only see him. "Blow job? What if you climb up here and sit on my face, just for a minute, as an experiment? You know, for science."

I laugh and shake my head. "Later, you can conduct scientific research. For now, you need to figure out the fine art of napping."

"How can I nap when you're here and so sexy and beautiful? I can't resist you, my little wildcat."

It's been a minute since he called me that. I like it now better than I did then. "Go to sleep and rest. You're worse than a baby right now. At least a baby can't talk back and try to fondle you."

He goes still, keeping a tight hold around my waist. I lie against him, remaining quiet so I don't keep him from napping if he's actually capable of stopping himself for long enough to sleep.

Michail slips into the room and leaves food on a small table across from the bed. How the hell is Kai supposed to reach it all the way over there? I climb off his obscenely large bed, retrieve the tray, and bring it to where Kai is pretending to rest.

He pops one eye open, then both when he sees the food. "Oh, he put the cheese I like on here."

I nibble on a white piece of cheese he shoves toward my face. "If Adrian's enemies only know how you can be brought low by cheese. They'd be buying stock, flocking to farms, who knows."

He sits up, and I allow it, so he can eat. "I don't know about all that, but if someone finds an extra sharp cheddar that is so sharp it almost burns, then I'd be a very happy man."

"You're so weird. How did I marry such a weird man?"

He kisses me, his breath smelling of the garlic cracker he popped in there a moment before. "Just lucky, I guess. You are also super lucky if Michail made this charcuterie tray."

I snicker and then laugh so hard tears leak from the corners of my eyes. "Charcuterie tray, really? Criminals excel at charcuterie?"

"I don't know about criminals, but Michail does. He's good at pairing cheese and cracker combinations."

I laugh again. "Noted, if we ever need another one."

He reaches out and brushes something off the side of my face. "We need a shower. We still have dried blood on us, and it's starting to feel a little crusty."

"Ew, gross." He quickly removes the IV, and I race him into the bathroom. Inside, I let him tug my T-shirt and black slacks off. Then my panties and bra. Once I'm naked, I do the same for him, and we climb into his giant rainfall shower together.

The water turns cold before we get out. After washing the blood away, we stayed under the water to explore each other a little better. It feels nice to be in his arms and not be constantly bombarded with worry.

I tug his mouth to mine, kissing him deeply, letting the now cool water mingle on our lips. "I love you. I hope you know that. Our marriage was never about saving you from the council. It was about something else."

I thread my fingers in his and lean into him. "You make me feel safe."

He caresses my cheek softly with a thumb. "You make me feel safe too. I love you more than I thought possible. I was unprepared for it, caught off guard, and if I'm being completely honest, scared enough that I wanted to push you away."

I hug him tighter, and then we climb out of the shower to dry off and get into bed again.

He whispers, "I love you," against my lips, and I fall asleep in the warm embrace of his arms.

Until his cell phone bounces off the side table, and he has to chase it down.

I want to throw the damn thing, but he answers, his tone guarded. "Hello?"

I can hear Selena's frantic voice screaming on the other end of the line from the bed. "Hey, big brother, it's time to call in that favor. I'm demanding sanctuary, and I'm going to need it right about now."

# BOUND TO CRUELTY

### Michail

Are we playing babysitter to every fucking mafia princess on the East Coast? I catch the last of Kai's phone call, waiting in the hall, knowing he'll request one of us to take care of this at any moment. With Andrea barely functioning and Alexei trying to defuse his sister, that leaves Ivan and me. Ivan is handling the family's day-to-day business at the moment. I'm the only one who can leave again at the drop of a hat.

Doesn't mean I want to race off and help Kai's sister, the very sister who was supposed to be protecting him in Chicago and left him and Rose to rot. She doesn't know the meaning of family and doesn't deserve our protection. So I'll wait, and I won't go unless Kai orders me to, and even then, I might have to think about it first.

Andrea marches down the hall, her dark hair swinging behind her in a shining mass. Today, she's traded her stilettos for black combat boots, which means someone might end up dead. Considering how active Sal's family still seems to be, and that's been her surveillance op, it looks like she's ready to take things into her own hands. Adrian told her not to make any moves yet, but I'm in favor of a good...culling. Those bastards need to be wiped out completely. From the grandparents who founded their empire on the blood of children to the cousins who may or may not be involved in the smuggling. I don't give a shit; they are all going down.

"Michail," Kai calls from his bedroom.

With a sigh, I step into the room and go find him. I have little doubt he's about to send me after his sister. I also have little doubt he won't take no for an answer, even if she seems like a spoiled little brat who doesn't deserve his help or mine.

But even though they share actual DNA, he and I are more family than they will ever be, and for that alone, I'll do what he asks. Hopefully, she'll comply and let me tuck her away into a safe house somewhere to hide until whatever she is dealing with blows over. With the season open, I suspect she's obviously not equipped to handle things. Someone must have tried a coup and succeeded if she called for an extraction and protection.

So where does that leave our council friends in Chicago then? A good question.

I run my hands through my curls, which are mussed and tangled from all the traveling and wrangling Kai's big body back in one piece. So I leave them instead and walk into Kai's bedroom to take in the scene of domestic bliss.

Rose is turned away, under the covers, asleep by the soft snores I can hear. I shift my focus to Kai. "You need something?"

"Yeah, I need you to go to Chicago and get my sister."

I clench my jaw and swallow. "Are you sure about that? She was supposed to be protecting you and didn't do shit, apparently."

Despite lying flat on his back in his bed with no shirt—no clothes at all, from what I can tell—his tone hardens. "It doesn't matter what she did or didn't do. I don't go back on my word, and if she needs help, she'll get it."

I sit on the edge of his bed, careful not to jostle his woman awake. "And what's your secondary plan? How do we keep things cordial with the Chicago council if you're taking her away just after their season opens? What if the new head of the council in her city doesn't take it so kindly?"

"Do I look like I give a shit about council politics?"

I sigh. "You should. We all have to play this game now, or each ripple in the pond will send back repercussions."

His gaze turns to ice. "I don't care about your fortune cookie logic. Go to Chicago, get my sister, and keep her safe. That is an order, and as an order, I expect you to follow it without question."

I level him a look. "None of us do, without question. You know that better than anyone."

He nudges his leg over to scoot me off the side of the bed. I stand and dance out of reach before he can do any damage. "I'll bring her back, put her in a safe house, and she'll be fine."

"No, that's not enough. Sit on her until she's safe."

I don't bother asking, why me. It would border too close to whining than I'm comfortable with. Instead, I face him, hands on my hips. "Are you sure about this? You want her here? Even after she didn't hold up her end of the bargain, and even though you two don't necessarily get along?"

He stiffens, then grimaces, settling back into his fluffy pillows. "Who says we don't get along?"

"The fact that none of us have met her or anyone in your family. That tells me straight up that either they are something you want to hide or something you don't think is an active part of your life. So, on that note, is there something about your family I should know, anything about your sister specifically?"

He snorts. "No, and the only reason I haven't introduced any of you is because I consider this my family. They are blood, but you, you are family. And as for my sister, she's a spoiled brat who loves power above all else. Don't let her get under your skin, or she'll burrow deep and cause actual damage."

I nod and then sigh. "Fine, I'll do as you ask, but you owe me."

His eyes narrow. "What do you want then?"

"I want off safe houses and moved to the casino. Alexei can take the safe houses for now; I have an idea about hiding your sister in plain sight."

"At the casino?"

"Why not? We might as well put her to work if she's staying with us."

He moves like he is about to sit up, then thinks better of it. "My sister will not be working the bars."

"Really?" I shake my head. "I'm not that big an idiot. I'm not going to make your sister whore for her room and board, for fuck's sake. Besides, we pride ourselves on women who actually want to be there. Something tells me working at all is a concept your sister is unfamiliar with."

"Just go."

I head toward the door but stop when he calls my name. I wait, listening.

"If you fuck my little sister, I'll kill you."

Wow. I shoot him a glare and don't justify that statement with a response. Like I have time to get my dick wet when every damn heiress needs a protector these days, and the Doubeck family seems to be intent on protecting them all.

No. Right now, all I have time for is packing my bag and calling to get the helicopter ready to depart.

I head to my room, throw open my closet to reveal my stash of weapons on one side, clothing on the other. Everything from tuxedos to rags. I've played many parts over the years. Many faces I've worn to secure Adrian's power. Today might call for something a little unconventional. At least until I get the measure of Kai's sister and what kind of danger she poses to us. I'll keep her safe, but only until the moment she puts Adrian and his power base at risk, then I'll face Kai's wrath, even if he chooses to kill me.

Once I land in Chicago, head to one of our safe houses there, and change, it's time to get to work. With her cell phone signal, the one she used to contact Kai, it's easy enough to trace her. I only hope she was smart enough to use a burner and hasn't contacted anyone else with it.

I find her on the corner of a busy intersection, black high-heeled boots clicking on the asphalt. Her hood is up, obscuring her hair, but by the way she ambles along, she doesn't seem too concerned. At least not out here surrounded by civilians.

I adjust the backpack on my back, pull the brim of my Chicago Cubs hat lower over my brow, and follow her and the mass of people into the subway. I'm very good at preparing for a stakeout. I've already loaded my metro card, and it's easy enough to follow her onto the platform. While she may be a small woman, five feet five in those boots, she has a presence of power about her I've learned to recognize in others.

She's going to need to strip that away too if she plans to stay safe out here in the open. Moving quickly, she gets on the train and finds a stance next to a doorway, her hand gripping the upper rail. I keep my distance, but my eyes are on her through the crowd. My black sunglasses ensure she doesn't see me looking at her.

After a moment, she turns her face toward me, and shocked she actually picked me out of the crowd, I touch the brim of my hat. This causes her to narrow her eyes and face out the window despite the fact it's pitch black in the subway tunnels surrounding us.

When the car slows, she shoves through the crowd to reach me, stopping at the door I've parked myself at. "If you are with them, tell them to fuck off and leave me alone. You won't kill me here in front of all these people."

I scan the crowd. "A knife to the gut takes seconds, and no one will see a thing except the student who tried to help you before the cops showed up, and he got scared."

Her dark eyes flare with something…anger? It's not fear. I know that much.

She leans in close, and I feel the barrel of a gun through her hoodie pocket. "Try it if you want, asshole, but you're going to have to get a lot of blood on you to keep me from taking a shot before you can get away."

I reach out and grab her hand, shifting the muzzle toward the crowd. "I'm not here to kill you."

"Oh, then what? I know they sent you, so are you here to what, bring me back, beat me up to scare me away, what?"

Her voice is low, and to anyone else, it might look like we are chatting, flirting even, so I lean into that, dipping my face so my mouth is near her neck. "I'm only here on surveillance at the moment, but the second it's time to do my job, I'll let you know first."

She swallows hard, and I catch a whiff of her perfume, something obscenely expensive and frivolous. "Fine, now unhand me. I have to get off."

I chuckle. "Well, I can't help you with that either."

She drags her eyes up to my face and then stops at the sunglasses. "You just made a comment about stabbing me, and now you are joking about giving me an orgasm. Wow. You must be some kind of psychopath."

I lean in again. "The best kind of person, in my opinion."

This earns me a curl of her lip, and she turns to face the door, her shoulder almost brushing my chest. "By the way, you aren't fooling anyone into thinking you're a student. Your shoes are too expensive, and that watch screams money. Next time, try a department store Timex if you want to blend in properly."

The train jerks to a halt, and she steps off onto the platform. I let her go, then follow with the crowd and keep my distance. She doesn't look back, even when she leaves the station and heads north on another crowded boulevard.

I stand near an alley and watch her walk up the steps to a brownstone, unlock the door, and go inside.

Then, I catch someone else peel themselves out of the shadows of her lower stairs and march up to the door. I wouldn't think anything of it except I'd just seen him. The same man helped us free Kai, one of our own council members.

What the fuck is he doing here?

**Order Bound to Cruelty Now!**

## ABOUT THE AUTHORS

**J.L. Beck** is a *USA Today* and international bestselling author who writes contemporary and dark romance. She is also one half of the author duo Beck & Hallman. Check out her Website to order Signed Paperbacks and special swag.

www.bleedingheartromance.com

∽

**Monica Corwin** is a New York Times and USA Today Bestselling author. She is an outspoken writer attempting to make romance accessible to everyone, no matter their preferences. As a Northern Ohioian, Monica enjoys snow drifts, three seasons of weather, and a dislike of Michigan football. Monica owns more books about King Arthur than should be strictly necessary. Also typewriters...lots and lots of typewriters.

You can find her on Facebook, Instagram and Twitter or check out her website.

www.monicacorwin.com

Printed in Great Britain
by Amazon